Assassins Of The Dead 4
King's Request

Assassins Of The Dead 4: King's Request

Avril Sabine

Cracked Acorn Productions
Australia

Assassins Of The Dead 4: King's Request

Published by

Cracked Acorn Productions

PO Box 1365

Gympie, Queensland 4570

Australia

978-1-925941-07-4 (Kindle)

978-1-925941-58-6 (EPUB)

978-1-925941-59-3 (Print)

Genre: Young Adult Fantasy/Paranormal

Copyright 2019 © Avril Sabine

Cover design by Caitlyn Petersen

*For my friends, my life is far richer for having
all of you in it.*

Some heroes work in the shadows, only their deeds remembered.

No one turns down a request from the king. No matter what it is or how dangerous it might be. Meikah needs to find a way to cover the real reason she needs to visit the capital and worries about how much longer she can continue to follow Kellan into mischief without her family doing something drastic. Yet how can she turn down the king's request? And does she even want to?

*

This story was written by an Australian author using Australian spelling.

Name Pronunciation

Like many names there is more than one way to pronounce the following ones. These are the pronunciations used in this story.

Amiel (ah-meel)

Branok (bran-ock)

Breena (bree-nah)

Cato (cay-toe)

Daveth (dav-eth)

Ena (en-ah)

Galzeren (gal-zair-en)

Garven (garven)

Isha (ee-sha)

Jelena (jell-en-ah)

Kellan (kell-en)

Letha (lee-thah)

Livia (liv-ee-ah)

Lorena (law-ren-ah)

Magan (mag-en)

Maksim (mack-sim)

Marta (mar-ta)

Meikah (mee-cah)

Mezeth (mez-eth)

Neven (nev-en)

Sarette (sah-ret)

Sirena (sigh-ren-ah)

Suri (sue-ree)

Timell (tim-ill)

Chapter One

Meikah drank in the sights around her. The Duke and Duchess' ballroom glittered. Not because of the ballroom itself, but from the guests in their finery. From the many jewels both the men and women wore that glittered in the light cast from bewitched flames.

Kellan spun her around the dance floor, one arm around her waist so that his hand was pressed against the small of her back while the other hand held one of hers. "Should I feel offended that you've not paid one bit of attention to me since we arrived?"

She smiled, her gaze meeting his. His black hair was tied at the nape of his neck and she saw humour in his brown eyes. Her other hand rested on his shoulder and she felt the muscles beneath her hand tense. "You're lucky I find this so interesting or I might fall asleep on my feet." She'd spent today and yesterday at the Spellsword Academy, relieved she'd managed to sleep through most of the day before yesterday. All that sleep hadn't helped her escape the lecture her parents had given her about the behaviour they expected from her at the ball. And their demands she stop spending time with Kellan and joining him on his pranks.

Kellan chuckled. "That would give the gossips something to talk about."

Her smile faded. "Is that why we're here? To create more rumours?"

Before Kellan could answer, a servant approached, moving around the floor with them as they continued to dance. "Excuse me, my lord."

Kellan came to a stop, keeping his arm around Meikah's waist and letting go of her hand. "Yes?"

The servant bowed. "The Duke would like to have a word with you, my lord." He nodded deeply to Meikah. "If you would excuse us, Miss."

Meikah nodded, drawing away from Kellan. No one declined a summons from the Duke or the Duchess. Not even Kellan would dare.

Kellan captured her hand, drawing it to his lips. "I'll be back as soon as possible. I had hoped to spend every moment with you." He grinned. "I'm sure you'll be able to find something to keep you entertained while I'm gone." He glanced past her before meeting her gaze again and grinning once more.

She looked over her shoulder, almost groaning when she spotted Cato. "What is he doing here?"

Kellan shrugged. "Looks like he's spotted you and is heading this way."

She nearly groaned again. "Not if I can help it." She tugged her hand from Kellan's and slipped through the crowd, heading towards an alcove that was partially hidden by potted plants. The scent of the large creamy coloured flowers enveloped her as she brushed past them. Scanning the crowd, she smiled when she saw Cato looking around, remaining where he was rather than heading in her direction. He'd obviously missed seeing where she'd gone. After the way he'd treated her, she didn't want to have anything more to do with him.

She observed the guests from her secluded location, smiling when she spotted her grandparents. Harlen was in his element. So was Sirena. Now if only Kellan could avoid causing any trouble she might manage to go an entire day without a lecture.

Two well-dressed ladies strolled past her hiding place, their figures glittering with jewels. The first one took out a fan, waving it lazily back and forth. "It is such a crush."

The second lady also took out a fan, snapping it open. "Could you expect anything else? Who would turn down an invitation to one of the Duke and Duchess' balls?"

The first lady lowered her voice slightly. "I was surprised to see Meikah here. Especially after all the rumours surrounding her."

"What can you expect? Running around with Kellan." The second lady snapped her fan closed. "And those ridiculous rumours about her being a necromancer. As if a foolish girl like her could be so powerful."

Meikah couldn't hear the other lady's reply, they'd moved too far from her. She sighed. It had been what she'd wanted. For no one to believe she was a necromancer. But she hadn't exactly wanted them to think she was some foolish girl instead.

A bat flew behind the plants and landed beside her to become Rafe. He nodded in the direction the ladies had taken. "It looks like the plan is working."

"I suppose."

Rafe moved closer, taking her hand. "Is something wrong?"

She shook her head. She would indeed be foolish if she let their words bother her. "Should you be here?"

Rafe grinned, continuing to hold her hand. "No one said I wasn't welcome."

Meikah laughed. "Have you given anyone a chance to say you aren't?" She glanced at the plants separating them from the rest of the ballroom. "Or did you fly straight over here to hide with me?"

"Danton asked me to collect you and Kellan. He didn't say it was urgent so it can wait until the Duke is finished with him." Rafe gestured towards the dance floor. "Would you like to dance?"

"What I'd really like is for you to tell me what Sarette said to you when we left Longview."

Rafe stared at her for a moment. "You would never choose to become a vampire, would you?"

"No."

"That is what she told me."

Meikah frowned. "Why couldn't you tell me earlier?"

Rafe smiled, one tinged with sadness. "Relationships never work unless both parties are vampires. She also reminded me of that."

"Oh." She wasn't sure what to say.

Rafe's sad smile momentarily returned. "I didn't mean to make you uncomfortable."

"It isn't that, it's just-" She broke off, ending the sentence with a shrug. "Sorry. I have nothing against vampires, I just don't think being one would suit me."

He cradled her hand in both of his. "You have nothing to apologise for." A smile momentarily appeared. "I am the one who should apologise."

"Why?"

"For asking for a kiss." He let go of her hands, placing his on her shoulders. "To say goodbye to what can never be."

She opened her mouth several times, but was unable to think of what to say. Her gaze was drawn to his lips. "Do you think a kiss will change my mind about becoming a vampire?"

Rafe chuckled. "I have no illusions about myself. If you could be so easily swayed, I wouldn't be so interested. No, this is about curiosity. And not wanting to regret that I never asked."

Again her gaze was drawn to his lips. "Curiosity." She certainly couldn't deny she had her fair share of that trait.

Rafe lowered his head, his lips close to hers. "One kiss only."

Her gaze was again drawn to his lips and she couldn't help thinking about when he'd fed on her. She raised a hand, automatically starting to touch her neck. At the last moment, she placed her hand on his chest instead. "One. Just one." She couldn't deny she was curious too.

Rafe's lips met hers and his arms wrapped around her, drawing her close.

She sank against his body, returning the kiss, her hands linking behind his neck as she clung to him. As the kiss continued, she was startled to realise her magic had risen to the surface, static crackling along her skin.

Rafe drew back slightly. "I didn't realise I would have regrets after all."

She stared at him, dazed for a moment. "Regrets?" It had been that bad?

Rafe's hands momentarily tightened around her. "Regrets that there will be no more." Letting go, he stepped back. "I can hear Kellan coming. I'll meet the two of you out the front." He moved towards the plants, changing into a bat to fly towards the nearest window.

Chapter Two

Meikah stared after Rafe, not so sure the kiss had been a good idea. Her fingers brushed across her lips. She was more than a little tempted to want a second one. But he was right. A relationship between them wouldn't work. She would never choose to become a vampire.

Kellan slipped past the plants, stopping in front of her. "Have you chosen?"

It took her a few seconds to answer. Her first thought had been to ask how he'd seen. She supposed when you could see in the dark there weren't that many shadows for people to hide in. "No. I was saying goodbye to something that could never be." And like Rafe, gaining a few regrets of her own.

Kellan grinned. "Does that mean-"

She held up a hand, taking a step backwards. "Don't go jumping to conclusions."

His smile didn't dim. "I noticed you didn't tell me no."

He would have to notice that. She kept her expression stern, fighting the grin that threatened to escape in response to his. "We have other things to deal with."

"Don't we always?"

She noticed that he sounded pleased, not annoyed by the fact. "What did the Duke want?"

He patted his vest. "To deliver a letter to his brother." He glanced in the direction Rafe had taken. "I take it Rafe wasn't here just to give you a kiss."

Her eyes narrowed. Before she could say anything, Kellan captured her hand, stepping closer.

"I'm sorry. That wasn't necessary. I have no excuse for acting like a jealous idiot." He paused a moment. "Why was Rafe here?"

"Danton sent him to collect us."

"Why didn't you say?" Grinning, Kellan took a step towards the plants, drawing her with him.

"I can't leave my grandparents here," Meikah protested.

Stepping past the plants, Kellan beckoned a servant over. "Give us a few minutes to leave and then inform Harlen and Sirena that their granddaughter has left and there's no need for them to do so."

"My lord-" the servant's protests ended abruptly when Kellan handed him some coins. "Yes, my lord." He bowed before moving away.

"Kellan-"

He interrupted her protests. "Do you want to stand around here arguing or do you want to find out what Danton has to say?"

She sighed. It would have been nice to get through one day without a lecture. Although today's lecture might be postponed until tomorrow considering how late it was. "I want to find out what Danton has to say."

Kellan gave a single nod. "Good. So do I." Keeping hold of her hand, he led the way through the castle.

They met up with Rafe out the front and strode down the road towards Fable. Meikah couldn't walk as fast as usual in her finery. "Did Danton tell you anything about what he wanted?"

Rafe shook his head. "Only that he needed to speak to the two of you."

Trying to walk faster caused her to stumble.

Rafe steadied her. "Do you want me to carry you?"

"I'll be fine." She thought wistfully of the boots she regularly wore, trying to ignore the memory of what it felt like to have Rafe's arms around her.

The rest of the walk was done in silence, the streets

around them empty. Livia met them at the front door, tugging Meikah inside the bookshop. The shelves were crowded with various sized leather bound books and there was a curtain across the doorway behind the counter. "Hurry. He won't tell us anything until you're here. Everyone is in the kitchen."

Kellan grinned. "I was thinking of getting out of my evening wear first."

Livia's eyes narrowed. "Don't even think about it." She let go of Meikah to grab Kellan's arm. "You can get changed after you find out why Danton received a letter from King Branok."

Kellan came to a stop, pulling out of her grip. "This is something to do with the King?"

Livia nodded. "At least I assume it is since he sent Rafe to fetch you after he opened it."

Rafe stood in the doorway behind Kellan, who was blocking the way. "That letter was from the King?"

Livia grabbed hold of Kellan's arm again, tugging him forward. "I recognised the seal."

Meikah looked back and forth from Kellan to Livia. "Why would the King send a letter to Danton? And not one to the Duke."

"That's what I want to find out." There was a slight growl to Livia's words. "Hurry up." Livia grabbed hold of Meikah's arm.

Meikah eyed Livia, half expecting her to shapeshift into her black mountain cat form. "Does he receive many letters from the King?" She took a step towards the curtained doorway, glancing at Kellan when he didn't move.

"What does a letter from the King have to do with us? Or does Danton need to tell us he has to go away for a week or two?" Meikah stumbled at Livia's side when the shapeshifter tugged her forward.

Livia drew Meikah around the counter. "He never goes anywhere. We're the ones that get sent places."

A thrill of excitement rushed through Meikah. She'd only ever been to the Arcton Mountains. "We're going to the capital? To Port Mayren?"

"I don't know. That's what I want to find out." Livia didn't let go of Meikah's arm until they were in the kitchen.

Meikah glanced around the room. The back door was closed and a pot of food bubbled gently on the stove, filling the kitchen with mouth watering smells. Everyone was there. Danton, Rafe, Shade and Mace. Even Amiel stood to the side, arms crossed over his chest and glaring at Danton. Meikah sat at the wooden table beside Mace, half tempted to ask Danton what was going on. But he would tell them when he was ready.

Kellan gave the letter from the Duke to Danton before he joined Meikah at the table while Livia dropped onto a chair opposite Meikah and next to Shade. "Now can you tell us what's going on?" Livia asked.

Before Danton could speak, Amiel did. "Not Mace. It isn't necessary."

Danton met Amiel's angry glare. "You would keep him locked away?"

"If you send him away, I go too," Amiel stated.

"Mace gets to go to the capital?" Livia asked. "What about the rest of us?"

Danton looked directly at Meikah. "We can't expect Meikah to travel there on her own."

Meikah stared at Danton, not sure she'd heard correctly. "I'm going to the capital?"

Danton inclined his head. "The King requests your help."

"How would he even know I exist?" It wasn't like her family were important. If it wasn't for Kellan, the Duke and Duchess probably wouldn't know she existed.

"He didn't ask for you by name," Danton said. "He asked for the dragon touched. I informed the commander at our headquarters in Port Mayren that one of our faction is dragon touched."

Meikah had no idea what to say. Her mind was blank. She stared at her hand where the outline of a dragon often formed.

"What has all this got to do with me?" Mace asked.

"Unnecessary plots to keep her identity hidden." Amiel gestured towards Meikah.

At the venom in his tone Meikah was glad of the distance between them. She looked away from Amiel, turning to Danton. "You don't want the King to know who I am?"

"There are others who shouldn't know your identity. That you are dragon touched. They could use it against you and the dragons." Danton glanced at Amiel. "Which is why I've come up with a plan to keep your identity hidden."

"I don't mind going to the capital," Mace said.

"What about me?" Livia asked. "I could go to the capital."

"I'm willing to go," Rafe said.

"You went on the last mission." Danton turned from Livia to Rafe. "Even if we didn't need someone who can walk in the daylight, I need your help here to make sure all is well with the local vampires after what they endured while the Society Against Vampires was here."

"Not Mace," Amiel stated. "The deal included keeping him safe. He stays in Dreyton."

"I can go."

When instant silence fell at Shade's words, Meikah glanced around the table. Everyone was staring at Shade. "Is there a problem with him going?"

Shade interrupted Livia's protests over him going. "No one will know I'm there. I'll be one more faceless Assassin Of The Dead."

Chapter Three

"Why shouldn't you go to the capital?" Meikah looked to Livia when Shade remained silent.

"A Dark Blade faction from the capital tried to take over the town Shade is from. He took down their leader while his family took out any of their high-ranking people. The leader's children warned Shade that they'd take him down if he ever returned to the area." Livia turned to Shade. "You can't go."

Shade smiled fleetingly. "They won't even know I'm there, Liv."

"If you go, I go too," Livia stated.

Danton shook his head. "Only one extra. Mace or Shade. Whoever it is, he'll be incognito when he accompanies Meikah and Kellan who'll go as themselves."

"I'll go." Shade glanced at Amiel. "Some problems are preferable to others."

Danton inclined his head before turning to Kellan. "My brother needs a reason to threaten you and Meikah with the school in the capital for wayward students. The one Meikah's grandfather threatened to send her to. I'm sure I can leave that task in your capable hands."

Kellan chuckled. "Absolutely."

Meikah was tempted to drop her head into her hands. "Can't we do anything that doesn't lead to me getting a lecture from my family?"

Kellan grinned at her. "You could always permanently move in here."

She sighed heavily. The option was looking more appealing every day. "When do we need to leave for the capital? And what exactly does the King need done?"

"You leave as soon as possible," Danton said. "And he never said. His letter states that he needs the services of the dragon touched. Nothing more, nothing less."

"Why the secrecy?" Meikah asked.

"Sometimes letters fall into the wrong hands." Danton rose from the table. "I'll leave you to your planning while I have Shade take a letter to my brother." He smiled. "And this time, do get caught."

Meikah watched him stride from the room. "I much prefer it when he tells us not to get caught."

Kellan rose from his chair. "I have the perfect prank. One I've been keeping for when I need to make a big impression."

This time Meikah did drop her head into her hands. "I'm never going to hear the end of this, am I?"

Kellan chuckled. "That's the point." He tugged her hands away from her face. "How good are you at climbing?"

She looked up at him. "Why?" She didn't bother keeping the suspicion from her tone.

Kellan tugged her to her feet. "It doesn't matter. It's not a big drop if you fall."

Before Meikah could protest Kellan's comment, Rafe spoke.

"Do you need help?"

Kellan kept hold of Meikah's hand. "No. We need to make sure only the two of us are caught." He gave a single nod to Rafe. "Thanks though."

"What do you expect me to climb?" Meikah demanded.

Kellan looked her up and down. "It'd be best if you could climb in that outfit, but if not, we'll take it with us. Much more effective if you're wearing your ball gown."

Meikah tugged her hand from Kellan's grip and crossed her arms over her chest. "I am not going anywhere until you tell me what the plan is."

Kellan grinned. "To get caught, of course."

Meikah breathed out heavily. "To get caught doing what?"

"But I want to stay and see what happens," Livia protested.

Meikah glanced over her shoulder to see Shade tugging Livia from the room, Mace following them. She returned to glaring at Kellan. "What is the plan? And don't go giving me only half of it."

"Remember the fountain the Duchess told us we weren't to go swimming in?" Kellan asked.

Meikah groaned. "We're going swimming in it."

"Of course we're not," Kellan said. "We told the Duchess we wouldn't."

"Then what are we doing?"

"Boating." Kellan strode from the kitchen.

It took Meikah a moment to gather her thoughts. She hurried after him, stepping into the bookshop. "Boating? The fountain isn't that big."

"I know." Kellan opened the front door, looking over his shoulder. "Can you climb in that ball gown?"

Numerous arguments went through her mind. She didn't speak a single one. The King needed her. The

King! She sighed heavily. It would be so much easier if she could tell her family. She frowned. No one had actually said she couldn't. "Does your family know?" She was tempted to smile when she saw it was Kellan who frowned this time.

"That I'm a necromancer? It's part of why they tolerate the rest of the rumours. They're preferable to the original ones. Is that what you meant?"

"No. Do they know about all this?" She made a vague gesture that encompassed Fable and its contents.

"No. It's better that they don't. Safer. It wouldn't take them long to put together who everyone else is. They'd never deliberately put any of us in harm's way, but the less people who know the less chance there is that the wrong people will learn anything."

"Is it a rule?"

Kellan returned to her side, letting the door close behind him. "The whole idea of a secret society or faction is that it remains secret from as many people as possible."

"The people know we exist. Or at least some of them do."

He captured her hand, tugging her close. "To most people we're myths and rumours. They have no face to put on the organization."

"What about Danton? Do people know he's part of the Assassins Of The Dead in Dreyton?" Her gaze was drawn to her hand in his. It reminded her of how close she'd been to Rafe earlier.

"They know him only as a contact person, not as a member. If his brother wasn't the Duke, he wouldn't know any more than my parents do." Kellan paused a moment. "Are you sure that was a goodbye kiss earlier?"

She met his gaze, remaining silent. She had no answers for herself let alone Kellan. It was meant to have been a goodbye kiss, but she couldn't get the thought of it out of her mind. This trip was probably just what she needed. Time away so she could think things over.

Kellan lightly squeezed her hand. "You're right. None of my business."

She started to tell him that hadn't been the reason she'd remained silent, but he continued speaking.

"Are you ready to go? It'll be easier to get caught if the ball is still going."

She nodded, following Kellan outside, letting him continue to hold her hand. Silence fell between them as they strolled along the road, remaining at a pace slow enough that Meikah didn't stumble in her finery.

They returned to the ballroom and Kellan took two goblets of wine from a passing servant, requesting another grab him a bottle. The protests ended when Kellan dropped some coins into the servant's hand. Kellan nodded towards nearby doors leading out into the gardens. "We'll be out there in the rose arbour."

Chapter Four

As they crossed the room, Meikah scanned it, looking for her grandparents. She didn't spot either of them. She didn't know if that was a good thing or not. Even if they weren't here, it wouldn't help. They'd soon hear about her latest exploits. She waited until they were outside before she spoke. "Why did you have to be so loud when you said we'd be in the rose arbour?"

Kellan grinned. "How else are the gossips to hear where we're going?" This time he kept his voice low.

"You want them to follow us?"

"How were you expecting us to be caught?"

Before Meikah could protest that there had to be a better way, the servant found them and handed over the bottle of wine.

"Thank you." Kellan turned to Meikah as the servant walked away. "How about we take this to the fountain?" He spoke loud enough that anyone nearby would have heard. Before speaking again, he lowered his voice and leaned close. "Protest. Remind me we were told not to swim in it again." He grinned. "And make sure you speak up clearly."

Meikah took a step away from him. "Are you serious? The Duchess warned us we were never to swim in the fountain again."

Kellan chuckled. "Did I mention anything about swimming?" He draped an arm around her shoulders, the wine bottle pressing against her arm, the goblets in his other hand. "I'm sure there are plenty of other things to do at the fountain." He strolled in the direction of the fountain, chuckling again.

Meikah lowered her voice. "I don't think they're following."

Kellan leaned his head close to hers. "It looks like you're right. Seems like they might be going to fetch an audience rather than follow us first to see exactly what we're up to. We're not going to have much time to get ready. The good news is that you'll get out of climbing over a wall. Bad news is that you'll be left behind to sort out the barrel and risk being caught alone."

"What barrel?"

"The Duchess objected to the Duke's dog drinking out of her fountain so she had a half barrel placed nearby and filled with water. You can tip the water out of it and put it in the fountain while I fetch an oar." Reaching the fountain, Kellan stepped away from her and placed the goblets and bottle of wine on the edge. "I won't be long." He gestured off to the left. "The barrel is over there."

He left before Meikah had the chance to spot the barrel. Finding it, she hurried forward, tipping the water into the garden bed behind it. The action was awkward in her ball gown and dancing slippers. After a great deal of effort, she managed to get the barrel in the fountain. The sound of running footsteps had her spinning to see who was coming. Kellan carried an oar, grinning when Meikah faced him. Reaching her, he handed it over and stripped off his jacket, placing it in the bottom of the barrel.

Meikah handed the oar back. "You do know it's not going to float."

"I know, but no one else realises that I do." He helped her into the barrel, joining her once she was seated.

They were pressed close together and it was impossible to move. "I hope we're not stuck in here for long."

Kellan rested the oar against the side of the barrel, the end of it in the water. He undid the top couple of buttons of his shirt before leaning forward and tugging some strands loose from her elaborate hairstyle.

She tried to brush his hands away. "What are you doing? It took me hours to have my hair done like this."

He wrapped an arm around her waist, his face close to hers, arranging a hand to partially hide her face. "They're approaching." He angled his head so those approaching would believe they were kissing.

She was conscious of how close he was to her, the kiss with Rafe coming to mind. "Kellan-"

He interrupted. "You could at least put your arms around me." His lips curved into a smile. "I also wouldn't protest if you wanted to make the illusion a reality. As long as it wasn't a goodbye kiss."

She slipped her arms around him, pressing her upper body against his. When his arm tightened around her, a crackle filled the air, her magic rising. Meeting his gaze, she saw the lightning in her eyes reflected back at her from his. Her lips parted. She had no idea how to answer him. Before she could come up with a coherent reply, a voice broke the silence.

"Meikah!"

Her magic dissipated and she wanted to close her eyes and sink below the lip of the half barrel. But it wasn't that deep. Somehow, she drew her upper body away from Kellan and met Harlen's gaze, unable to miss seeing the shock in his eyes. The shock quickly turned to anger. It was a good thing necromancers couldn't die.

Kellan picked up his goblet from where it sat on the edge of the fountain. He raised it in a toast to the Duchess who stood at the front of the crowd. "Would you care for a drink, Your Grace?"

"Did I not say you were never to swim in my fountain again?" the Duchess demanded.

Kellan took a sip from the goblet before placing it back on the edge of the fountain. He raised the oar. "I'm not. I'm taking Meikah for a paddle around the fountain. Although I'm afraid I've discovered a barrel doesn't float very well. Otherwise, I'd offer to take you once around the fountain, Your Grace."

The Duke pushed through the crowd, stopping beside the Duchess. "Up to mischief as always I see, Kellan."

Kellan rose to his feet, drawing Meikah up with him. He bowed. "Your Grace, have you considered boats for the fountain?"

"No, but I have considered sending you to the capital so you can see exactly what the school for wayward students is like. Maybe it will make you think twice about getting up to one of your pranks in future," the Duke said.

Kellan chuckled, picking up and raising his goblet to the Duke. "Good joke, Your Grace."

"It's no joke," the Duke said curtly. "I'll expect to see the two of you tomorrow morning. At seven." He offered the Duchess his arm and the two of them strolled away, most of the crowd following them.

Meikah stared after them. She felt dazed, half excited and had a great deal of dread pooling in the pit of her stomach. She was going to the capital. To see the King. Who had specifically asked for her. Well, maybe not her specifically, but she was the dragon touched.

Kellan leaned close. "How do you want to play this?" He glanced at Harlen who was approaching.

"I don't know." She supposed running wasn't an option. Especially not while wearing dancing slippers.

Kellan helped her out of the barrel and onto the paving stones that surrounded the fountain. He nodded towards Harlen. "Evening." He grinned. "Or is it morning?"

Harlen glared at him. "I think you've said more than enough. And I think you've spent more than enough time with my granddaughter."

Kellan draped an arm around Meikah's shoulders. "That is not your decision to make." He turned his head. "Meikah?"

She drew in a shuddering breath, her legs feeling like they might give out on her. Somehow she met Harlen's gaze. The warning in them made her raise her chin. "I was thinking we don't spend enough time together. Not with how much time I waste each day at academies that don't really want me attending them."

Harlen stepped forward, grabbing hold of Meikah's arm and dragging her away from Kellan. "It's past time for you to go home."

Kellan took a step forward, his hand dropping to the hilt of his dress sword. "Meikah?"

Chapter Five

Meikah looked from Harlen to Kellan several times before shaking her head. She didn't want them fighting. That wouldn't end well. She forced her lips into a smile. "I'll see you in the morning when we visit the Duke."

Kellan held her gaze a moment longer before inclining his head.

Looking over her shoulder, as Harlen tugged her back towards the castle, she saw that Kellan watched her as she walked away. She tried to smile reassuringly, but he didn't return her smile, only continued to watch her with his hand resting on the hilt of his sword.

Stumbling, she faced forward, glancing over her shoulder when she felt mist brush her cheek. This time the smile came more easily when she saw Kellan followed at a distance. She wanted to tell him she was fine, but didn't want to draw Harlen's attention to him.

The carriage was waiting out the front for them, Sirena seated inside. The drive home was silent, the lecture not starting until they were inside and Heron and Breena were present.

Meikah stood silently for a moment, caught up in thoughts of what the capital might be like. All she knew about it was that it was in the middle of a natural harbour and one of the first settlements of their country. Would the Duke expect them to attend the school for wayward students or did he only plan for them to visit? And who would accompany them that far? There was no way her parents would allow her to travel that distance with only Kellan for company. Even with a masked guard accompanying them.

"Meikah!"

At Heron's sharp tone, Meikah turned to her father.

"Have you heard a word any of us have said?" Heron demanded.

She doubted telling him she hadn't would be a good idea. "I need a few hours sleep if I'm to see the Duke at seven." She headed for the stairs in the shocked silence.

"Are you going to let her get away with speaking like that?" Harlen demanded.

Meikah started up the stairs, not wanting to stick around to find out the answer to her grandfather's question. She'd barely reached the top of the stairs before an argument broke out down below. She didn't wait around to learn the outcome. Reaching her room, she closed and locked the door behind her, leaving the candle unlit. She didn't need light to change her clothes and find her way to bed. Even before she had the ability to use magic to see in the dark she hadn't needed to light a candle to find her way around the house she'd been raised in.

She'd barely crawled into bed when a sound had her looking towards the window, her magic brightening the area so she could clearly see Kellan climb inside. She sat up, watching him cross the room.

He looked her up and down, also able to see in the dark with the help of his magic. "Are you unharmed?"

She nodded. "He wouldn't physically hurt me." At least she didn't think he would. These days she wasn't completely certain about anything. Not with how much everything had changed.

Kellan sat on the edge of the bed beside her, taking hold of her hand. A smile fleetingly appeared. "I can't help wondering if you would have made the illusion a reality if we hadn't been interrupted so quickly."

A smile reluctantly formed. She had hoped to keep a straight face when she answered him. "I guess you'll just have to keep wondering."

Kellan chuckled softly. "I'll collect you in the morning on the way to the castle." Letting go of her hand, he rose to his feet.

"I don't know if that's a good idea."

"I'm pretty sure it isn't." With another grin, Kellan climbed out the window and was gone from sight.

Still smiling, she lay back down. She was going to the capital. The thought struck her again, bringing with it the thrill that had barely formed earlier. It was slowly starting to sink in properly. The King needed her. Still thinking about it, she sank into sleep, waking to a light knock on her bedroom door, her room still filled with the shadows of early morning.

"Meikah? Are you awake, Meikah?"

She stumbled from bed at her sister's persistent knocking, barely managing to open her eyes. She partially opened the door, leaning against it to stare at Ena. "I'd rather I wasn't."

"Did you really swim in the Duchess' fountain again?" Ena took a step into the bedroom.

Meikah pushed away from the door, facing the room as she tried to decide what to wear. "No."

"Then why are you in so much trouble?" Ena asked.

Meikah took out a pair of trousers and a shirt. She had no idea what to expect, but considering Kellan was involved, anything was possible. "We tried to go boating in the fountain."

"You did what?" Ena demanded.

Meikah looked up from the clothes she'd laid out on the bed, chuckling at Ena's expression. "In a barrel and with an oar and two goblets of wine."

"You were drunk?" Ena asked.

"No." She returned to the doorway. "I need to get ready for the day." She closed the door on Ena's protests, forcing her sister to step back out of the way.

It didn't take long to dress and Meikah headed downstairs for breakfast, ignoring Ena who'd waited for her, asking far too many questions. She was shocked to see Harlen had joined them for breakfast. Not that he ate much. He spent most of his time glaring at her and arguing when she tried to leave the house without him. She made it as far as the door, but he blocked her exit. She kept glancing past him to the open doorway. Pushing past him wouldn't go well.

Kellan turned up partway through the argument. "Are you ready to go?"

"She is not going anywhere with you," Harlen stated.

Kellan chuckled softly. "I think you'll find the Duke has other plans. Such as the two of us travelling to the capital together."

Harlen took a step towards Kellan, pointing a finger at him. "You will stay away from my grandaughter. This behaviour is all because of you. We didn't have any of these problems until she started socialising with you."

Kellan shrugged. "You're not the first person to accuse me of being a bad influence."

She wasn't about to let Kellan take the blame after all the help he'd given her in changing the direction of the rumours. "I was the one who sought him out and the one to join him in his escapades. None of this is Kellan's fault." She squeezed past Harlen. "I need to see the Duke. I doubt he'd be impressed if I was late."

Kellan draped an arm around her shoulders. "Keeping him waiting is never a good idea."

"Meikah!"

She ignored Harlen's call, focusing on the road ahead. She had no idea how to stop him from following and could only hope the Duke wouldn't be annoyed to find she had a chaperone with her.

At the castle, they were ushered towards the throne room, Harlen as well. The Duke rose from his throne at their approach. He looked first at her and then at Kellan. "The two of you follow me."

"Your Grace-" Harlen broke off when the Duke looked at him.

Meikah hurried to the Duke's side, wishing she had the ability to quieten her grandfather so easily. She followed the Duke into a side room, surprised to find Isha seated in front of a desk that was set in one corner.

The Duke gestured to the chairs beside Isha. "Take a seat. Both of you."

They did as they were bid, sharing a look as they sat down. Meikah wanted to ask the Duke why Isha was there, but she remained silent. Kellan probably would have asked, but she didn't know the Duke as well as he did.

The Duke looked at each of them before speaking. "The Duchess is rather unimpressed with last night's antics. Or should I say earlier this morning's antics? She wanted a more harsh punishment for the two of you. Luckily, I need a cover story for one of my operatives to travel to Port Mayren." His gaze rested on Isha. "Your husband has always been loyal to me. I assume I can expect the same from you?"

Isha nodded. "Of course, Your Grace."

"You will accompany your granddaughter to the capital. You are, after all, the most logical choice. Harlen and Sirena have many duties to attend to while her parents have another child in their care."

Meikah barely managed not to smile. Ena would not have been impressed to have heard the Duke call her a child. Especially since she was the oldest of the two of them.

"Can you be ready to leave in two hours?" the Duke asked Isha.

"Certainly, Your Grace," Isha said.

"The carriage will call for you then." The Duke indicated the door.

Isha rose to her feet, glancing at Meikah and Kellan.

The Duke looked sternly at both of them. "They may go once I've told them what behaviour is expected of them during the journey."

Isha curtsied before leaving the room, closing the door behind her.

Chapter Six

Silence filled the room and Meikah glanced wistfully at the door. She was fairly certain that no matter what the Duke said, Kellan would follow his own rules.

Kellan grinned at the Duke. "You have to admit, it was an inspired prank. We didn't swim in the fountain."

The Duke sighed, slowly shaking his head. "I think you gain far too much enjoyment from your cover stories, Kellan. The Duchess is also of the same opinion."

Kellan chuckled. "You could be right, Your Grace." He stretched out his legs, leaning back and making himself more comfortable in the chair. "What task do you have for us? I doubt you're about to waste your breath on telling us how to behave." Kellan grinned.

The Duke sighed again. "No wonder your parents worry over you."

Kellan's grin remained in place.

Meikah eyed the distance between her and Kellan, wondering if his foot was close enough that she could kick it without drawing the attention of the Duke. Was he trying to get into more trouble?

The Duke rose from behind his desk, having taken a letter out of the top drawer. He held it out to Kellan. "Give this to the commander of the Assassins Of The Dead in Port Mayren. I'll need you to remain in the capital long enough to not only complete whatever task the King might have, but to wait for a reply to the letter."

Kellan tucked the letter away. "Consider it done, Your Grace."

The Duke gestured towards the door. "The carriage will collect each of you after it collects Isha." He waited until they were nearly at the door before he spoke again. "Kellan."

Kellan turned to face him. "Yes, Your Grace."

"You might not want to use the fountain in any more of your pranks. The Duchess was extremely unimpressed."

Kellan inclined his head. "I'll keep that in mind, Your Grace."

"I should hope so." The Duke paused a moment. "Tell Harlen I wish to see him."

Meikah stepped out of the room and nearly ran into her grandfather. She wished now that she'd thanked the Duke for wanting to see Harlen. She interrupted his whispered tirade. "The Duke wishes to see you."

Harlen stopped mid-sentence, looking past her to the open door. "Now?"

Meikah nodded, escaping the moment Harlen stepped inside and closed the door. She waited until they were outside before she spoke. "How long will we be in the capital? What will I need to take with me? Do I take…" Her voice trailed off as she glanced at the guards. She lowered her voice. "Those other outfits."

Kellan nodded. "Always. You never know when we might need them." He shrugged. "As to how long we'll be gone, who knows."

"I've never been to Port Mayren before. Where will we stay?"

"I have a relative we can stay with. An uncle. He's a bit of a recluse, but as long as we don't expect too much from him, he won't mind us staying."

Meikah glanced at Kellan. "All of us? Shade too?"

Kellan nodded. "All of us, but Shade will probably

stay at the headquarters." He paused a moment. "Make sure you pack evening wear. Uncle Garven expects his guests to dress for dinner. You might want to take your ball gown too. You never know what entertainments will be happening while we're in the capital."

"I don't have evening wear," Meikah protested.

Kellan grinned. "Yes, you do. The two dresses I gave you."

And there was the answer to the question she'd been worried about asking. She wasn't sure how she should feel. While she was still trying to decide, they arrived at her home.

Kellan drew her back to him when she would have headed inside, his hand resting at the small of her back. "Are you all right? You're not worried about heading to the capital are you?"

She hadn't been until now. "Should I be?"

Kellan grinned. "Not at all. I've been there before. I'll show you around once we've finished our tasks. There's a lot to do. You'll love it."

Before she could protest, not sure the mischief she saw in his eyes boded well, he was striding in the direction of Fable. She sighed heavily. What sort of trouble was he likely to get them into in the capital? She supposed she was about to find out. Heading inside she stopped abruptly when she saw her father waiting for her. She tried to ignore the concern she could see in his eyes. It didn't help that she had her own worries and concerns.

"What did the Duke have to say?"

She didn't answer immediately. "The carriage will be here to collect me in less than two hours. He's sending me to the capital to see what's in my future if I'm not careful."

"Meikah!"

At the hushed exclamation, Meikah turned to see Breena by the window. Had she been watching for her arrival?

"What have you to say for yourself?" Heron demanded.

Meikah remained silent. There wasn't a single thing she could say.

"Well?" Heron took a step towards her.

"I need to pack." She fled upstairs before she said something she shouldn't, ignoring her parents calling out to her. Reaching her room, she stopped in the doorway, surprised to find her sister packing a trunk. "What are you doing?"

"That hooded one said the Duke was sending you to the capital. I answered the door." Ena smiled wryly. "There was no way I was going to pass that message along."

Meikah laughed softly. She didn't blame her sister.

Ena placed a handful of undergarments in the trunk before turning to face Meikah. "He brought two dresses to pack." She paused, as if waiting for a reply. When Meikah didn't speak, she continued. "What have you been up to, Meikah? Where did the clothes come from?"

"They were a gift."

"A gift like that doesn't come without strings," Ena warned.

Thinking of Kellan, Meikah smiled. "Not everything comes with strings." She added the ball gown to the trunk.

"I hope not." Ena stood back, hands on her hips as she surveyed the room. "I think that's everything."

Meikah stared at the trunk. She was going to the capital. A shiver ran through her. She'd never been anywhere important. What did she know about the capital?

"Oh, Meikah." Ena came forward, resting her hands on Meikah's shoulders. "I don't think you have a choice about going."

"I didn't say anything." She stepped back from her sister.

"You didn't have to. I saw it on your face." Ena came forward again and rested a single hand on her shoulder. "We're templars. We come from a long line of templars. There is nothing we can't face."

She met her sister's gaze, seeing in it the faith Ena had in their family. She started to say she was a necromancer, changing her mind at the last second. Nodding, she stepped back. She knew more about being a templar than she did about being a necromancer.

"Good." Ena turned to the trunk. "Let's get this closed and I'll help you carry it downstairs." She shut the lid. "I can't believe you're getting to go to the capital after all the trouble you've caused. It's more like a treat than a punishment."

Laughter burst from Meikah. "I suppose it is."

Ena eyed her up and down. "How did you manage it?"

She shrugged. "I think it's Kellan's fault. If it was only me, I'd probably be grounded for life and never see the outside of my room."

"Probably." Ena hefted one end of the trunk by the handle.

Meikah took hold of the other handle and headed downstairs, going backwards down the steps. They left the trunk by the front door and she looked around, not seeing her parents. She was tempted to remain by the door and leave without speaking to them.

Chapter Seven

Sighing, Meikah went to look for her parents, finding them in the kitchen, arguing in whispers.

They broke off when she entered, Breena putting a plate of food on the bench. "You'll want something to eat before you leave." She nodded towards the food.

Not knowing what else to do, Meikah helped herself to the food.

"We have a distant cousin who lives in Port Mayren that you can contact while you're there, if you wish," Breena said.

Meikah nodded, her mouth full.

"See Lorena if you have any problems," Heron said. "You could stay with her. She wouldn't object."

Again Meikah nodded.

"The Duke should have allowed us to go with you," Breena said.

Meikah was glad she'd had another mouthful and

couldn't comment. It was difficult enough to meet their gazes without needing to lie to them about what was going on. She'd begun to think she'd get away with continuing to eat and occasionally nodding. That was until Harlen and Sirena turned up with their lectures and demands as to what she'd been thinking.

Finishing her meal, Meikah shrugged in answer.

"What do you mean you don't know what you were thinking?" Harlen demanded.

"Surely you didn't follow along with no thought to the consequences," Sirena said.

Meikah glanced at the exit. Why hadn't she asked to be collected first?

"The Duke should have sent us with you," Harlen said. "Isha won't keep you out of trouble. She's as likely to encourage you."

Meikah bit her lip in an effort not to smile at that comment. It was probably the truth. She edged towards the doorway.

"It might be better to send her to the school for wayward students instead of letting her return home," Sirena said.

Meikah moved a little closer to the doorway. There was no way she was going to remain in the capital if that was to be her fate. And she doubted that Isha would agree to leave her there.

"Sirena-"

Harlen interrupted Breena. "I don't know how she ended up like this. Ena doesn't give us any trouble. Look at how well she's doing with her training. She's a credit to the family."

Meikah judged the distance between her and the doorway. It was too far to make it before anyone could stop her. She moved a little closer when everyone looked at Ena.

"I can't imagine what everyone must be thinking," Sirena said. "The gossip going around is terrible."

Meikah managed not to point out that it had to be better than the previous gossip. The doorway came closer and she moved a little faster.

"Where do you think you're going?" Harlen demanded.

"Port Mayren." The smile she'd contained earlier escaped as she fled through the doorway and towards the front door, ignoring everyone's demands to return. Flinging the front door open, she stopped when she spotted Kellan across the road, leaning against a tree as he watched her place. Hearing the voices coming closer, she slipped outside, closing the door.

Kellan met her on the edge of the footpath. "I

assumed there'd be trouble when I saw your grandparents arrive."

"How long have you been waiting out here?"

"Come to Fable. Rafe wants to say goodbye."

"That's why you're here?"

He shrugged. "I said I was going to see if you needed rescuing from your family. Rafe asked me to deliver a message since it's daylight."

She glanced over her shoulder, surprised to see her father blocking the doorway. "All right. Let's go."

Kellan chuckled as he fell into step with her. "I thought you'd prefer that." He nodded in the direction of her home, glancing over his shoulder as he did so. "Heron surprised me."

She nodded. Just like he'd surprised her. "What is Port Mayren like?" Anything had to be preferable to talking about her family and she did want to know what to expect.

"Busy."

When he didn't elaborate, she remained silent, enjoying the peace after the arguments and lectures she'd endured lately. They'd barely stepped inside before Livia was drawing Meikah behind the counter, telling her how lucky she was. Before Meikah could say anything, Rafe joined them in the hallway.

"Could I talk to you for a moment?" Rafe gestured towards the stairs leading to the basement.

Nodding, she followed him down the stairs, stopping at the bottom. "I thought you'd be in bed by now."

He smiled fleetingly. "I wish I could go with you."

"That would have been nice."

"Would it?"

She frowned, not sure what he meant.

"I was worried you might prefer to avoid me after earlier."

"The kiss."

He inclined his head.

She tried to think what to say.

"It's all right." Rafe took a step away from her.

She reached for him, placing her hand on his arm. "I'm not sorry, but it will probably take a bit of time for me to stop thinking about it."

"I didn't expect…" His voice trailed off.

"Neither did I."

He took her hand, holding it a moment before raising it to his lips. "I'll see you when you return from the capital."

She nodded, waiting until he let go of her hand before she moved back. She met his gaze a moment longer before she turned and hurried up the stairs, still not sure what else she could have said to him. It felt like they'd left a lot of things unsaid.

Livia waited in the hallway, full of things she wanted Meikah to see for her and tell her what they were like. She drew Meikah into the light-filled kitchen.

Meikah looked longingly at the back door. It seemed like all she wanted to do today was escape.

Kellan stepped between Meikah and Livia. "Give her a break." He grinned. "Or you'll have her running out of here too."

Meikah was relieved when Kellan explained the comment and she was left in peace, the conversation turning to other topics until the carriage arrived, having already collected her trunk.

Danton entered the kitchen as Meikah and Kellan were about to leave. He looked at each of them. "Don't get caught."

"I never do." Kellan grinned. "Unless it's planned."

They headed outside amidst goodbyes. There was a single driver and their luggage was strapped on behind the carriage and on the rack on the roof. Behind the carriage, mounted on horses, were four men in outfits similar to what the Assassins Of The Dead wore, their faces hidden. Meikah stood on the footpath marvelling over the coming journey. She was going to Port Mayren. After having never left the place of her birth for so many years, she could hardly believe she was about to go on another journey.

Entering the carriage, Meikah found Isha was already seated facing the front. She sat behind her, smiling when Kellan entered and looked first at her and then at the space beside him on the seat. She gave a slight shake of her head to let him know she didn't plan to sit next to him.

Shade joined them in the carriage, wearing an Assassins Of The Dead travel outfit, and Isha eyed him up and down as the carriage moved off.

At first, Meikah spent her time looking out the window, excited at the prospect of seeing the capital. It didn't take long for the journey to become monotonous and she sat back, drifting off to sleep, something she'd certainly been lacking lately.

The day was uneventful and they stopped in a small inn on the outskirts of a town, as night approached, heading off early the next morning. They would arrive in the capital an hour or so before dark, with plenty of light for her to see the city, if the journey continued to remain uneventful.

Chapter Eight

They were still a couple of hours from the capital when they were attacked, six masked riders coming out from amongst the trees and demanding all their valuables. Meikah reached for the sword and dagger she wore.

"No, Meikie." Isha grabbed Meikah's arm, trying to draw her back onto the seat.

Meikah shrugged Isha's hand off her arm, following Kellan and Shade out the door. Four of the bandits remained on their horses while two stood on the ground, swords held ready. No one moved.

"We have two more amongst the trees with crossbows," one of the mounted bandits warned.

Meikah eyed the bandit who'd spoken, her voice and figure giving away that she was female. "How do we know there are more with you?"

A bolt flew towards the ground at Meikah's feet,

before it reached its destination, a gust of wind knocked it backwards.

Meikah glanced at Shade, who held two daggers. Wind was his element. She grinned when two of the mounted masked figures murmured to each other. "Doesn't look like having another two with you will help."

"Ride on and you may go free today," one of the guards, accompanying Meikah and her companions, said.

A man mounted on one of the horses, laughed. "You think you can keep that trick up against all of us attacking? I doubt it."

"One way to find out." Kellan stood beside Shade, his sword and dagger ready.

"You're a spellsword?" the woman asked.

Kellan shrugged. "I know a couple of tricks."

"You better hope it's more than a couple." The woman attacked before she'd finished speaking.

Meikah instantly went into action, her dagger knocking a bolt from the air while she swung her sword at the other masked figure standing on the ground. Lightning flared along her blades and she drove the figure back into one of the horses that reared, throwing the rider from its back.

Around her the guards attacked, Kellan fighting at

her side and Shade disappearing amongst the nearby trees. She didn't know if she should follow him to help. Then it wasn't an option. One of the guards was pinned to the ground and she dashed past the masked figure she fought to help the guard. She attacked his opponent, her own opponent following to join in the fight. Her blades slashed through the air. Blocking, attacking and occasionally getting past their defences.

Magic crackled through her, continuing to encase her blades. For once the dragon outline didn't form on her hand, but then she didn't feel overly threatened by those she fought. Which surprised her. She hadn't realised how much she'd improved with all the practice she'd been getting. Disarming one of her opponents, she focused on the other one for a moment, disarming them only to find that the first opponent had picked up their sword. Before she could attack them again, the ground beneath them darkened and they slipped in mud as they started to move forward.

Kellan laughed. "Guess those few little tricks are enough after all."

Meikah surveyed the area, the lightning crackling around her weapons. All their attackers were scattered across the ground, most of them smeared in mud from trying to rise to their feet. Annoyance arrowed through her and it took her a moment to realise it was aimed at Kellan for ending the fight. She'd been holding her own. She hadn't needed his help.

Then it dawned on her. It wasn't about the fight. It was about the magic coursing through her that had nowhere to go. When one of the masked figures tried to rise, she channelled some of the lightning towards them.

The bandit yelped, dropping back into the mud puddle Kellan had created.

Seeing another one trying to rise, Meikah did the same to them. This one snarled, trying again to rise, reaching for their sword as they did so. She sent more lightning towards them, careful not to send too much their way. This time they remained down, glaring up at her. The annoyance she'd been feeling faded, along with the amount of magic coursing through her. A smile formed. She was starting to get the hang of her magic. Although she doubted Amiel would be impressed with her progress. The past two days he'd had nothing but complaints.

Isha hurried to Meikah's side. "You weren't injured?" She looked Meikah up and down.

"No."

Isha tugged her towards the carriage. "We'll get out of the way and let the guards secure the bandits."

Meikah sheathed her weapons and allowed Isha to draw her back to the carriage. She caught sight of a bolt embedded in the side of the carriage below the window. A rush of anger went through her. "You weren't hurt?" She started to turn away, taking a step towards the bandits.

Isha drew her back. "I was on the other side of the carriage." She opened the door and clambered inside, sitting on the seat that faced forward. She patted the leather of the seat beside her. "Come join me."

Meikah checked that everyone was safe before she did as Isha bid. Shade had returned with two prisoners and Kellan was helping the guards secure the others. "What is wrong?"

Isha examined her. "You were never meant to be a templar. Whatever you've become since you learned you're a..." Her voice trailed off and she glanced out the window, lowering her voice before she continued. "A necromancer. Whatever it is, that is what you should be doing. You loved every minute of that fight. And it isn't your first fight. What you did out there, you didn't learn in any academy."

Meikah held Isha's gaze. "No, I didn't."

Isha smiled, patting Meikah's hand. "You don't need to tell me what it is. Just know that I'll stand by you, whatever it might be."

"It isn't-" Meikah broke off, trying to think of the right word. "Evil. It isn't evil."

"I never would have expected it to be."

Kellan joined them in the carriage, sitting across from them. "That was a welcome bit of exercise after so long in the carriage."

Shade entered the carriage, sitting beside Kellan without a word.

"Where are the bandits?" Meikah looked out the window as the carriage moved off.

"Tied and slung over their horses. The guards can deliver them to the guardhouse when we reach the capital," Kellan said.

Isha looked at each of them. "You've all fought together before."

"What makes you say that?" Kellan asked.

"Grandmother Isha-"

"You don't have to say anything." Isha patted Meikah's hand. "Who would I say anything to, anyway?"

Kellan grinned. "In that case, if anyone asks, we've never fought together before."

"Is anyone likely to ask?" Isha met Kellan's gaze. "Or is that an answer for me?"

Kellan shrugged. "You never know who might ask

what question or what rumours the answers might lead to."

Isha again patted Meikah's hand, meeting her gaze, this time saying nothing.

Meikah smiled at her grandmother, giving her a single nod. She wasn't sure what she was trying to tell Isha, but the nod cleared the worry from Isha's eyes and Meikah settled back in the seat, looking out the window again.

The fight had slowed them down and they didn't reach Port Mayren until the sun was setting. The guards rode off with the prisoners while the carriage continued towards Garven's house.

Meikah stared out the window, watching all the people on the streets and the many horses and carriages on the roads. Kellan had been right. The place was busy. They headed towards an older neighbourhood with sprawling houses that overlooked the ocean. The house they pulled up in front of looked weathered and in need of repairs. It was silent and nothing moved. She half expected to learn it was deserted.

Kellan stepped out of the carriage, helping first Isha and then Meikah down. "Inside isn't as bad as outside. Uncle Garven is a little strange. He doesn't trust anyone to work on the house and isn't capable of doing the repairs himself."

Shade silently followed them to the front door, scanning the area. He kept his voice low when he spoke. "Let me know when you're ready to return to Dreyton." He turned to Kellan. "You know where I'll be staying."

Chapter Nine

Meikah wanted to protest when Shade slipped away, the shadows momentarily hiding him from her view. Now she could see in the dark, it didn't take her long to use that ability to watch Shade move out of view. She nodded towards the front door. "Are we going to let your uncle know we're here?"

Kellan nodded, knocking on the door as he did so. He glanced at the carriage. "Once Isha is settled, we should visit the school. Get it out of the way."

Before Meikah could protest that she didn't want to go anywhere near the school, the door swung open. The man who answered looked them up and down, his expression remaining impassive. She felt like they'd been assessed and found severely wanting.

"I suppose you're expecting to stay," Garven said. "As inconsiderate as that fickle son of the King's."

Kellan grinned. "Hello, Uncle Garven. Mother said to tell you to be nice for a change."

Garven snorted, stepping back so they could enter. "Make yourself useful while you're here and listen to the housekeeper's complaints about the prince so I don't have to. Does she think I care about all the drama? Don't even remember the name of the first girl he's no longer spending time with. Or the vindictive piece of work he's now keeping company with. No one would have anything to do with her if she wasn't the daughter of the Sorcerer Academy's director."

Isha entered the house, glancing around. "Sounds like you know more than you'd have us think you do."

Garven glared at Isha. "What can you expect? She natters away about it from sun up to sun down."

Kellan made the introductions and told the carriage driver to bring the luggage inside.

"He can leave it in the foyer," Garven said. "No need for him to traipse all through the place." He started to walk away, glancing over his shoulder and pausing before stepping through a doorway. "Don't go expecting me to run around after you and don't upset the housekeeper. You know where everything is."

Meikah stared at the empty doorway. "Should we stay somewhere else?"

Kellan chuckled. "Not at all. He's delighted to see us." He made a gesture towards the doorway Garven had disappeared through. "I'll show you to your rooms and see if the housekeeper has enough food prepared for all of us."

Meikah eyed Kellan. "Do you know what the word 'delighted' means?"

Kellan chuckled again. "This way." He showed each of them to a room upstairs, lugging the trunks up for them.

Meikah stood at the window of her room, looking out at the ocean, a few lights bobbing in the distance. She opened the window and the scent of salt reached her. The place was nothing like home. A tap on her open door had her spinning to face it, her hand starting to go towards her sword. She stopped the action when she saw Isha in the doorway.

"You aren't really going to visit the school this evening, are you?" Isha asked. "Wouldn't it be better to wait until morning?"

"I suppose." Meikah smiled. "But we might have a walk around and explore the place a little."

"Port Mayren isn't like Dreyton. I know you're capable of facing a fair fight, but here you'll find thieves hiding in the shadows and all sorts of nefarious people wandering about. Wait until morning," Isha said.

Meikah wanted to protest. The King had requested her help. Before she could argue, Kellan joined them, standing behind Isha who turned to face him.

"Good news. The housekeeper will feed us. The meal will be ready at eight." Kellan held out his hand to Meikah. "Want to join me for a walk along the beach?"

"I really don't-" Isha began.

Meikah hurried forward, slipping past Isha to take Kellan's hand. "It's the beach. I doubt there'll be thieves hiding in the shadows on the beach."

"You never know what to expect in the city," Isha warned.

Meikah tugged Kellan towards the stairs. "An hour. We'll be fine." She kept moving.

"One hour only." Isha followed them. "You know Harlen would never let up if I allowed something to happen to you while we're here."

Meikah let go of Kellan's hand to dash back and hug Isha. "Nothing will happen and Harlen will have nothing to complain about."

Isha's arms tightened around her. "I want you to

enjoy yourself while we're here, but be careful while you do. This place is absolutely nothing like home."

Letting go of her grandmother, Meikah took a step back. "This isn't my first time away from home, Grandmother Isha. Port Mayren can't be any worse than the Arcton Mountains."

"One hour," Isha stated.

Nodding, Meikah spun and grabbed Kellan's hand before hurrying downstairs. She waited until they were outside before she spoke. "When are we going to see the King?"

Kellan strode towards the beach. "Shade plans to notify him of our arrival once he's delivered the Duke's letter to the commander."

"I wonder what the Duke wants of the commander," Meikah said. "Why couldn't Danton have helped him?"

Kellan shrugged. "Might be looking for information." He shrugged again. "It could be anything. It might even be about the Duchesses' niece. He could be making sure the King's son will be good enough for her. Although that looks like it might not be an issue now."

Meikah laughed. "Why wouldn't the King's son be good enough for her? He's a prince."

Kellan slowed to a stop and faced Meikah. "Do you think that's all it takes? Prestige?"

She met his gaze, her magic making it easy to see his expression. Not that it made it any easier for her to figure it out. "No."

He stared down at her for a moment before he grinned. "Good." He faced forward again and continued walking.

Meikah remained at his side. "Why is it good?"

He glanced at her, only grinning in answer.

She started to ask him again, shaking her head instead. "How long will it take for Shade to arrange a meeting with the King?"

Kellan shrugged. "He may already have arranged one, or he could still be waiting to see the King. But at least if we make it easy for him to contact us by walking on the beach, we should find out sooner rather than later." He made a sweeping gesture, indicating their surroundings. "In the meantime, why not enjoy this nice romantic walk with me?"

"It's not at all romantic."

"Are you sure? What about the moonlight on the water? The soft breeze off the ocean? The expanse of white sand stretching out before us?" He indicated each thing he named. "Or do you object to the company?"

"You know it isn't that."

Kellan didn't answer immediately. "Do I?"

This time it was her who brought them to a stop. She stared up at him for a moment, her words soft when she finally spoke. "We work together." She wasn't sure how she'd be able to work with Rafe again. At least not without thinking about the kiss.

Kellan rested his hand on her hip, stepping close. "How is that a problem?"

Chapter Ten

Meikah stared into Kellan's eyes, seeing the lightning in her own reflected back at her from his. She placed a hand on his chest, trying to tell herself to push him away. Beneath her hand his heart beat a little faster than usual and her plans to push him away evaporated. Her gaze slowly lowered, momentarily resting on his lips before returning to his eyes. "It's a terrible idea." The words sounded thoroughly unconvincing.

Kellan chuckled, raising the hand he still held, to his lips.

"Kellan-" Her protests died the moment his lips were pressed against the back of her hand. The air crackled around them as her magic rose. She started to move in closer, a sound causing her to pull away instead. Like Kellan, she reached for her sword, lowering her hand when she saw Shade approached.

"Nice timing," Kellan said dryly.

Shade inclined his head. "It could have been worse."

Kellan chuckled. "Possibly." He paused a moment. "Have you seen the King?"

Shade inclined his head again. "He wishes to see you as soon as possible."

Meikah glanced in the direction of the house. "How am I expected to manage that without letting Grandmother Isha know what's going on?"

"Retire early for the night?" Kellan asked.

Meikah slowly shook her head. "No, she'll know something's up if I do that."

"We wait until she retires for the evening," Kellan said.

"What if that's too late?" Meikah asked.

"The King didn't say immediately," Shade said. "He only said as soon as possible."

Meikah again glanced in the direction of the house. "We should probably go back. We're only meant to be gone an hour. I don't want to worry Grandmother Isha."

"I'll return for you in a few hours," Shade said.

"She rarely goes to bed before ten," Meikah warned.

With a single nod, Shade strode away.

Meikah watched him go for a moment before she turned towards the house. "I wonder if the King told Shade why he wanted to see me."

Kellan slipped his hand in hers as they headed back towards the house. "He would have told us if the King had mentioned something like that."

The two of them fell silent, Meikah's gaze regularly drawn out to sea where a scattering of lights bobbed up and down. She had one more look at them, glancing over her shoulder before she stepped inside, wondering about who was out on the water and what it was like on a ship. She'd never been on one before. Or even in a boat. A slight smile formed. And the barrel in the fountain certainly didn't count.

Evening passed slowly and the meal was a silent affair with Garven glaring at them down the length of the table. He retired the moment the meal ended, telling them they could entertain themselves.

Kellan grinned. "My uncle has always been the perfect host." He rose to his feet. "I should write a letter to inform my parents of my safe arrival. If either of you need paper, you'll find it in the study."

Meikah pushed back her chair. "I should probably do the same."

Isha gathered up dishes. "I'll take these to the kitchen and give the housekeeper a hand."

Meikah followed Kellan to the study, taking the paper and nib pen he held out to her. She glanced around the room, looking for somewhere to sit while she wrote her letter. The only chair was behind the desk and Kellan was using it. The rest of the room was taken up by shelves of books arranged by height and colour rather than subject or author.

Kellan looked up from the letter he was writing, shifting across on the chair with a grin. He patted the small section of the seat when she didn't move.

"I can wait until you're finished." She wasn't certain if she should risk the temptation of sitting so close to him.

Kellan chuckled. "Are you sure?"

She wasn't sure of anything lately. Keeping that thought to herself, she nodded, sitting down the moment he vacated the chair. Once her letter was written, Meikah prowled the house, waiting for it to be late enough that she could slip out to visit the King without being noticed.

In the end, she grabbed a book off the shelf and used that as an excuse as to why she was going to bed early. She dropped a kiss on Isha's cheek, starting to step away from her.

"Don't fall asleep with the candle on," Isha warned.

Meikah grinned. "I don't need a candle these days."

Isha laughed softly. "I'm glad you're learning how to not only live with your new abilities, but to make them yours."

Meikah stared at Isha, stunned. She hadn't thought of it that way. Slowly nodding, she smiled before making her way upstairs, a book clutched in her hand and numerous disjointed thoughts racing through her head. It didn't bother her like it used to. Being a necromancer. Without it, she'd never have met Danton and most of the other assassins and she wouldn't have travelled to the Arcton Mountains, which had eventually led her here. Her smile remained in place as she lay down, leaving the candle off. Life was far more interesting now she was an Assassin Of The Dead.

She nearly fell asleep, waiting for enough time to pass that she could slip outside. Sitting up in a rush, Meikah set the book aside and dressed in her Assassins Of The Dead travel outfit before making her way to the window. It didn't take her long to spot the best way down and she was on the ground seconds before Kellan who was dressed similarly to her. "Do you know where-" She broke off as Shade stepped out of the shadows along the side of the house.

"Are you ready?" Shade asked. When they nodded, he led the way to where a carriage awaited them.

Meikah peered out the window as it took them through the city, drawing around to the back of the castle where they exited the carriage. It left the area the moment they were on the footpath. She stared up at the castle that towered over them. It was far more impressive than the Duke's castle, but she supposed it should be since it belonged to the King.

Guards met them before they'd gone far and after Shade explained who they were, they escorted them to a small room at the back of the castle, Shade unable to enter with them. Meikah couldn't stop staring at everything, several times nearly running into things as she followed the guards. It still amazed her that the King had requested her help. She didn't feel important enough to be someone the King would turn to.

The guards stepped out of the room, one of them stopping in the doorway for a moment. "Wait here. Someone has been sent to inform the King." He closed the door.

Meikah didn't know if she should continue to stand or sit at one of the eight timber chairs that were placed around the large table that took up most of the space in the room. "What are-"

Kellan interrupted her, nodding towards a grate

above a bookcase on the far wall. "We're being watched."

She stared at the grate, trying to see into the area behind it. A soft sound came from it and she smiled as she caught a glimpse of movement. "What do they think we're going to do?" The door opened as she spoke and she spun to face it.

A well-dressed man entered the room followed by a dozen guards that positioned themselves around the room. He had a neatly trimmed beard, that was a mixture of reds and browns, and close cropped hair. "They're always concerned about assassination attempts."

Meikah stared at him for a moment. He looked too ordinary to be a king. He looked more like a soldier. She started to curtsey when she noticed Kellan bowed, changing it into a bow when she remembered she wore trousers rather than a dress. It was odd meeting the King for the first time in trousers. Not that she'd ever expected to meet him.

Kellan straightened. "Your Highness." He gestured towards Meikah. "The dragon touched."

The King strode to the head of the table and sat down, indicating that the two of them should also take a seat. "How does one prove they're dragon touched?"

Meikah doubted a shrug would be a sufficient answer, but she'd never had to prove it to a human before. She had no idea how to go about it. "Dragons can easily tell."

"So I have no way to know that you're who you say you are unless I take you to a dragon," the King said.

"You can trust our faction. Surely that's enough," Kellan said.

The King remained silent for a moment. "We captured a dragon who was terrorising the countryside. She's been locked away since all she wants to do is destroy. I would hate to have to kill such a creature when I've made it illegal for others to do so. When I told the dragon I was bringing a dragon touched to speak to her, she spoke for the first time. She told me I lied. That there are no dragon touched left in the world."

Chapter Eleven

Meikah's heart sank. She had hoped that somewhere she'd find other people like herself. Ones who'd be able to tell her what it meant to be dragon touched. "If you take me to her, I can prove to both of you I am dragon touched."

Again the King remained silent, looking them over. "You'll need to leave your weapons behind. I can't risk you taking them to the dragon. I won't have her think you're a threat."

Kellan grinned. "With or without actual weapons, we're still armed and dangerous."

"Does that mean you refuse to come with me if you can't bring your weapons?" the King asked.

"We'd never refuse an order from you, Your Highness," Kellan said. "I'm just making sure you understand that taking away our sword and dagger won't make a difference to our ability to fight."

The King glanced at his guards before speaking. "You're spellswords?"

"You could say that."

Meikah was glad Kellan answered the King. She had no idea how he stayed so calm. But she supposed he'd had years of practice talking to the Duke. "Your Highness." She swallowed hard when he looked at her. "Dragons don't like being lied to. Leaving our weapons behind and trying to appear as if we aren't capable of fighting might be considered a lie."

The King once more remained silent for a moment before he rose to his feet. "Wait here."

Meikah stared at the closed door when the King and his guards left. She wanted to ask Kellan what they were meant to do now, but was conscious of the grate above the bookcase. Did someone still watch them? She looked between Kellan and the door several times, wanting to demand how he managed to look so relaxed. Had he met the King before?

Just when Meikah was about to demand how much longer they were expected to sit there, the door opened and a guard beckoned them forward. The two of them followed the guard and Shade, who'd been waiting outside, fell into step with them. This time they were escorted to the dungeons.

Meikah's hand automatically rested on her sword

and she lowered it as soon as she realised what she was doing. A glance at both Kellan and Shade showed that neither of them seemed bothered by their location. What had happened to the King? Where had he gone? Could his guards be trusted? She hated not knowing what was going on.

The guard in the lead unlocked another door, using one of the large keys on the bunch he carried on an iron loop. He stepped to the side and gestured them through.

Meikah hesitated. It was another lengthy corridor with yet one more locked door at the end.

"This is as far as I can go. Knock when you reach the other end and you'll be let in," the guard said.

"Who will let us in?" Kellan asked.

"The King awaits you." The guard once more gestured along the corridor.

With a single nod, Shade led the way.

Meikah followed at a slower pace, glancing over her shoulder at Kellan who walked behind her. She still didn't say anything, not sure who, or if anyone, was listening in on them.

Shade knocked on the door at the other end of the corridor. There was a scraping sound in the lock before it swung open. A guard stepped back to let them through and the King waited for them in the mid-sized room.

Meikah followed Shade inside, glancing around. In the far corner was a small table and two chairs, four goblets and a jug sitting on the table. Off to her left was another door, a shuttered grate in both the top and bottom of it. At hearing the door close behind her, she turned to watch the guard lock it. Her automatic protests died when she glanced at the King.

He gestured towards the table. "There's wine if you want any. Help yourself. There are no servants down here."

Meikah was pretty certain the guard would act as a servant if the King needed him to. "Where's the dragon?"

The King nodded towards the other door. "You'll need to talk to her through the grate. It's too dangerous to enter. She's been chained to the wall on the far side of the cell to help reduce the risk of her killing anyone that tends to her."

Meikah lowered her gaze, taking a deep breath before she looked up at the King again. "That won't work. I need to get close to her."

"That's madness," the guard blurted out. He cleared his throat, bowing to the King. "Sorry, Your Highness, I didn't mean to interrupt."

"Think nothing of it." The King made a dismissive gesture with his hand. "I couldn't have worded it any better myself. It is madness to enter her cell."

"Madness or not, it's what I need to do for her to see I'm dragon touched," Meikah said.

The King eventually nodded. "I'll assume you know what you're doing."

Meikah nearly laughed. Somehow she kept a straight face, fearing laughter would have ruined any chance of her being able to enter the cell. "If someone could open the door when I raise my hand." She stepped into place, trying not to think about what she was about to do. It wasn't like she had that much experience with dragons.

"The door will need to be closed once you're inside," the King warned.

"Do you need us with you?" Kellan asked.

Meikah desperately wanted to say yes. She forced her lips to curve into a smile, hoping it looked more natural than it felt. "I need to do this on my own." She turned to the King. "I understand." She understood a little more than she wished. If things went wrong, no one would let her out and risk the life of the King. Trying not to think about how she felt, Meikah faced the door and slowly raised her right hand, palm towards herself. When the door opened, she froze in place for a moment at the sight of the dragon chained at the other end of the far too small cell, a larger door to the right also closed and likely locked.

The dragon lifted her head, anger filling her eyes. Her mouth started to open.

Doubting the dragon was opening her mouth in greeting, Meikah hurried forward, keeping her hand raised. "I'm dragon touched."

The door slammed shut and was locked as the dragon smiled at Meikah. "Liar." With a roar, flames poured from the dragon's mouth.

Fear raced through Meikah and her magic rose around her. Before she could do more than turn her hand as if to push the flames from her, a lacey dragon met the flames, vanquishing them. Meikah stared open-mouthed at the dragon who had a similar expression of shock on her face.

The dragon grabbed hold of Meikah's hand, the warmth of her breath rushing over the back of it. The silhouette of a dragon in flight appeared on the back of Meikah's hand. Neither of them spoke. Both of them stared at the dragon silhouette as it faded.

"Who marked you?" the dragon demanded.

Meikah drew her hand away from the dragon, lowering it. "Letha."

"She still lives?"

Meikah nodded.

"What did you do for her?"

"I saved the life of her unborn child."

The dragon didn't speak immediately. "You need to make them let me go. You can't call yourself a protector of dragons and allow them to keep me chained here like this." The dragon rattled the chains that kept her imprisoned against the wall.

"The King isn't about to let you go so you can continue to attack the countryside. He's not unreasonable. That's why he sent for me. So the two of you can come to an arrangement." At least Meikah assumed that's why she'd been sent for from the little the King had told her.

"I want whoever killed my mate and then I'll consider discussing other things with your King." Steam rose from the dragon's nostrils. "Whoever it is, will be made to suffer."

Chapter Twelve

A shiver ran through Meikah at the tone the dragon used. "Maybe you better tell me everything. I can't exactly help if I don't know what's going on."

A knock on the door interrupted the dragon. She growled, glaring at it.

"Sorry. My friends are probably worried about me." Meikah gestured towards the door. "Give me a minute to let them know I'm well."

The dragon growled again. "No wonder I have little time for humans. They might be willing to harm those sworn to protect them, but dragons are not that stupid. Let them in if you must."

"Can I let the King in? It would probably be easier if he listened to what the problem is. He's the one I need to convince to set you free." Although Meikah had no idea how she could do that considering the dragon was determined to kill someone.

There was another knock on the door.

"Your friends are impatient," the dragon said.

Meikah smiled. "My friends are protective."

"I would like to meet those a dragon touched calls friends. I'd be interested to see who you think worthy of the term." The dragon made a rumbling sound. "And if you must let in the worthless human king, you may inform him he's safe from me for now. As long as you are here in the room with him and he or his people do me no further harm."

"Thank you." Meikah stepped over to the door, knocking lightly on it. "You can open the door now." She waited until it was open, smiling reassuringly at Kellan, before she gave the King the dragon's terms.

The King inclined his head, interrupting the guard's protests. "I'm interested in learning why the dragon attacked my people."

"Should I bring a chair for you and the King?" Kellan grinned.

Meikah could have done without the reminder of a dragon's tendency to take far too long to discuss anything. "That shouldn't be necessary." Realising she'd answered for the King, she turned to him. "I mean, it won't be necessary for me. Did you want a chair to sit on, your Highness?"

The King chuckled. "As you said, it won't be necessary."

Meikah entered the cell first, Shade and Kellan coming in to stand one on either side of her. The King joined them, waving his guard back.

"What do they call you, other than King?" the dragon demanded.

"Those close to me call me Branok. All others tend to call me King, Your Highness, or sire."

The dragon made a deep, rumbling sound. "I am not and will never be considered close to you. What do your enemies call you?"

"Do you consider yourself my enemy?" the King asked.

"I certainly don't consider myself a friend," the dragon said. "What else does that leave?"

Worried they'd end up with things in a worse state, Meikah spoke before the King could, even though she wasn't sure interrupting him was a good idea. "You never told us what to call you."

"You may address me as Mezeth." The dragon nodded towards the King. "He may address me as Ancestor Mezeth."

Meikah drew in a sharp breath. The dragon was one of the ancient ones? One of the handful most dragons were descended from?

The King gave the dragon a shallow bow. "My apologies for your terrible accommodations, Ancestor Mezeth. Maybe you've spent the past few decades in another country, but in this one, dragons aren't hunted and those who hunt them are hunted by the law."

"By whose order?" Mezeth demanded.

"Mine," the King said.

"It is about time." Mezeth inclined her head. "But that doesn't change anything. Someone killed my mate."

"You were going to tell us what you know about that, Ancestor Mezeth," Meikah said. "Do you know who it was?"

"How would I know that?" Mezeth demanded. "I've spent the last four decades hibernating. And I've already told you to call me Mezeth. You're my protector. It's your right."

Meikah started to speak at the same time as the King did. She broke off abruptly, turning to him when he didn't continue to speak. "I'm sorry, your Highness. You were saying?"

This time it was Mezeth who interrupted the King. "No. I will not allow it to continue. Dragon touched are above the laws of humans and as such are equal to rulers. Stop lowering yourself and addressing him in that way."

"Ahh…" Meikah looked between Mezeth and the King, not sure what to say.

The King smiled at Meikah. "You may call me Branok. I would like to hear the rest of this story."

"Thank you." Meikah could have told him that dragons always took their time with stories. Both in the telling and the listening. Not wanting to offend Mezeth, she kept the words to herself as she faced the dragon again. "Where did you last see your mate?" Remembering Mezeth had said she'd been in hibernation, Meikah added, "And when did you last see him."

"Fifty years ago. He was mortally wounded and his only hope of recovering was to go into hibernation. It wasn't far from here that he was attacked. I arrived in time to slaughter those who would have killed him and helped him to a nearby cave where I pulled the arrows and sword from his body. Once I was certain he was safe in the cave, and well hidden, I went to set our affairs in order before I too went into hibernation." Mezeth made a humming sound deep within her chest, but other than that she fell silent.

"You went into hibernation," Meikah prompted.

"It takes time to set dragon affairs in order. These

things are complicated. It was near on a decade before I could go into hibernation myself, planning to wake up a few weeks earlier than my mate so I could be waiting for him when he woke. As he would have done if it had been me who'd been wounded." Mezeth fell silent again for a moment. "That was if he did wake."

Meikah frowned. "He didn't make it?"

Mezeth growled. "If that were the case, his remains would have been in the cave and it would not have been opened. The sword I'd drawn from his body, and the arrows, lay mostly buried in the sand that coated the floor of the cave. Yet there was no sign of my mate. No marks of where he would have lain, no bloodstains from his wounds and no scales that had fallen from him when I removed the weapons from his body. There were, however, signs of a struggle."

"Dragon parts are valuable on the black market," the King said. "Someone may have found his dead body and taken it away to sell to those unscrupulous enough to make potions or spells from dragons. You don't know if those signs of struggle are recent."

Snarling, Mezeth rose to her feet to tower over them. "I want his body returned to me. No human is entitled to so much as a claw of his."

"I'll send guards and soldiers to discover what happened to your mate," the King offered.

"We'll seek answers too." Kellan grinned at the King. "There are places we can search that your guards and soldiers can't."

The King inclined his head. "I'd appreciate that." He turned to Mezeth. "Are you happy with these terms?"

"That remains to be seen. It will depend on if you discover what happened to my mate. I would also have whatever was made from his body, destroyed. We also have the matter of my accommodations. I am completely dissatisfied with them. Set me free immediately," Mezeth demanded.

"Do you promise not to attack my people?" the King asked.

Mezeth lowered her head so she was face to face with the King. "I will tear limb from limb any who get in my way. Your human laws mean nothing to me."

"We have laws to-"

Mezeth interrupted the King. "They obviously don't work. Someone killed my mate."

"All we know is that he's missing," the King said. "And that at some time in the past there was a struggle."

"Killed or kidnapped. It makes no difference. They all deserve to die for their actions." Steam curled up from Mezeth's nostrils, growing thicker.

Chapter Thirteen

Worried the King might be hurt, Meikah moved closer, placing her right hand on Mezeth. "What if the-" She broke off, swallowing hard before she continued. "Branok provides better accommodations for you while we see what we can learn about what's happened to your mate?"

"You expect me to stay in here?" Mezeth turned her glare on Meikah. "Are you not dragon touched? I've made allowances since you're some sort of magic wielder rather than the warrior they typically are, but even you should know better than to expect me to remain imprisoned."

Meikah wanted to protest that she had no idea what being dragon touched meant, but now was probably not the time to mention it. "I was actually thinking he should provide a safe place for you to stay in case there are humans in the area who are deliberately going after dragons. The less people who know you're here, the less likely any who hunt dragons would learn you're staying in Port Mayren."

A deep rumble rose from Mezeth's chest. "You think I can't protect myself?"

Meikah drew in a slow breath, holding back the words she really wanted to speak. "I'm trying to protect you. I'm not from this city and I don't know who or what is in the area or how dangerous it is. I want the chance to find out before you leave the dungeons. Can't we make some arrangement that will allow you to stay here unchained and with what you need to make the place comfortable and both of you agreeing not to harm the other?"

Shade stepped forward before anyone could speak, standing close to Meikah. "What if we promise to bring those responsible for taking your mate to you, or bring you to them?"

Mezeth turned her gaze on Shade. "That I can agree to. They are mine. Those who take from me will learn the error too late to mend their ways."

A shiver ran through Meikah at the threat in Mezeth's voice. She wanted to protest.

"If they've killed your mate, you can have them to do with as you will," the King said. "If they've taken the deceased body, then they belong to me to punish them under my laws. If you can agree to that, and the other terms, I can agree to all of them too."

"If it takes more than a week, our agreement is broken," Mezeth warned.

Meikah wanted to argue that it wasn't enough time. Before she could, the King spoke.

"I agree. One week." He held out his hand.

The dragon placed her paw over his hand, smoke curling upwards from her nostrils. "One week." She lowered her paw. "Now remove these chains."

Meikah wanted to close her eyes. Wanted to beg for more time. "Where is the cave?"

"I can fly you there," Mezeth offered.

"No." The word burst out of Meikah. At Mezeth's menacing glare, she tried to speak more calmly. "You need to remain out of sight. If you tell me where it is, we can travel there ourselves and have a look around."

"I could see the top of the castle towers from the island," Mezeth said.

"We need a map," Kellan said.

The King inclined his head. "I'll have the guard bring one along with the keys."

When a map was brought to the cell, Mezeth waited until the guard had left before she spoke, the guard having also given the keys to Meikah since the dragon had refused to allow him to approach her.

While her chains were removed, she pointed to an island out from the coast with a claw. Beside the island was written the words 'Durnning Island'.

"The waters around Durnning are dangerous," the King warned. "Very few can navigate them without their boat being dashed upon the rocks."

"That's a good start. It should make it easier to find out who discovered the cave." Kellan folded up the map. "Where abouts on the island is the cave?"

"On the far side, looking out to the horizon," Mezeth said. "There was a tumble of boulders hiding the entrance, spilling onto the sand. On the rise above them was a tree stump that had been uprooted by a storm, larger than a horse, the rest of the tree having been struck down decades ago by lightning."

Meikah rested her hand high up on Mezeth's forearm, the scales warm beneath her palm. "We'll keep you informed about what we learn."

Mezeth inclined her head. "Thank you dragon touched."

Meikah wanted to protest the name. She nodded, turning away to follow the King from the cell, Kellan and Shade walking with her. They remained silent until they were outside, the King breaking the silence.

"I'll tell my people to give you what help you need."

"Thank you." Meikah waited until the King inclined his head and strode away, surrounded by his guards, before she turned to Kellan and Shade. "Where do we start?"

"At the docks," Kellan said.

"I'll see what the assassins know," Shade offered.

After arranging to meet back at the house at daybreak, or leave a message under a rock by the back door if plans changed, they went their separate ways. Meikah was glad of her ability to see in the dark as they approached the harbour. Several taverns were still open, light and laughter spilling out onto the cobblestone streets, as well as drunken patrons who stumbled out to weave their way along the street. In alleys and pressed against buildings were hooded figures that warily watched them as they passed, hands hovering near sheathed daggers.

Meikah continued to scan the area, her magic rising around her ready for if she should need it. She also noticed several spirits, but they seemed more lost than looking to cause trouble so she ignored them. She wanted to move closer to Kellan, but doubted that would be a good idea. Not if they needed to fight. "What are we looking for?" She kept her voice low, her gaze continuing to scan the area.

"A smaller sailing boat and someone about at this hour. It might take a while. They could still be out at sea," Kellan said.

Meikah tried not to yawn, but it was difficult. How was she going to explain to Isha her need to sleep all day? Or at least a good part of the day. It would have been easier if they could have travelled to Port Mayren on their own. Like they'd travelled to the Arcton Mountains alone.

"There's one." Kellan led the way along one of the timber docks stretching out into the ocean. Several ships were moored along it, smaller ones close to the shore, the sizes growing larger the further they went along it until there were two larger ones at the end. They stopped halfway along the dock where two men unloaded barrels from a thirty foot sailing ship.

One of the men looked up, straightening when he noticed them. "What do you want?"

"We're looking for information." Kellan drew out some coins, taking more out one at a time until the man nodded.

"What sort of information?" the second man asked.

"Who could take us out to Durnning Island?" Kellan handed over the coins.

"What do you want to go there for?" the second man asked. "Nothing out there but sand and rocks."

"Has anyone been out there in the past decade?" Kellan asked.

The first man shrugged. "Not likely. Nothing out there. Used to be a meeting spot for smugglers, but they got better places to go to now."

"Used to be a place to bury the dead you don't want found is more like it," the second man corrected.

The first man shrugged again. "Probably still is for all I know."

"Does anyone still know how to get out there?" Kellan drew out another coin, tossing it in the air.

The gaze of the second man followed the coin. "Shorty. If anyone can get out there, it'd be him. He's been sailing this area since he was a babe." He caught the coin when Kellan tossed it to him. "Don't know what you want with Durnning though. It's a bad place. They reckon it's haunted."

"Nah, not haunted," the first man said. "Cursed. The place is cursed and unlucky. Probably all the dead buried there in unholy soil. They'd be restless, wouldn't they?"

Kellan drew out another coin. "Where would I find Shorty?"

"He don't come around here. He's got a place at the

end of Seaview Road. Don't like no one going out there either." The second man caught the coin.

"Is he known by another name?" Again Kellan took out a coin, running it through his fingers.

The first man shrugged. "Probably did once. But it'd have gone to the grave with his ma, decades ago."

Meikah wanted to ask how old Shorty was, but the first man pocketed the coin and turned back to his cargo.

"We gotta get this unloaded before sunrise."

"Thanks for your help." Kellan gave them a nod before turning towards the harbour.

Chapter Fourteen

Meikah walked beside Kellan, wanting to ask him if the night seemed quieter. It didn't take her long to spot several hooded figures trailing after them. A scan of the area had her counting the ones she'd spotted. Eight hooded figures followed them.

At the start of the dock, Kellan turned to the left, away from the noise of the taverns and towards darker and quieter areas.

"What are you doing?" If the hooded figures hadn't been so close she would have told him they needed to head towards crowds, not away from them.

"Finding a nice quiet place to ask a few questions." Kellan grinned, his hand resting on the hilt of his sword.

Dread settled over her. How were the two of them meant to take on eight attackers? Or possibly more. For all she knew there were ones she'd missed spotting. "You can't be-" She broke off when a hooded figure stepped out in front of them. Her hand automatically went to her sword. Nine. She hadn't spotted this one trailing them.

"Can you tell us how to find Seaview Road?" Kellan left his weapons sheathed.

"Nothing out that way other than Shorty. What do you want with him?" the hooded figure demanded.

"A lift to Durnning Island," Kellan said.

"Only the dead get a lift out there." The hooded figure drew two daggers. "How about we help you with that?"

Meikah drew her weapons at the same time as Kellan, glancing around at the rest of the hooded figures that were closing in on them. Nothing else stirred and the decrepit warehouses that lined the ocean front were closed and quiet. Her grip tightened on her sword and dagger when she counted twelve opponents with a variety of weapons. She wanted to protest. How were they meant to face so many at once?

Shade stepped out from beside a building, both his daggers drawn. A strong breeze proceeded him, chasing sand across the ground and swirling a handful of leaves about. "You might want to rethink this."

The hooded figure laughed. "You think one extra will be enough?"

Kellan chuckled. "More than enough." His dark blue blades slashed through the air as he attacked the hooded figure, mist curling across the ground towards him.

Meikah joined the fight, lightning crackling along the blades of her weapons, her magic filling the air around her. The hooded figures attacked and there was no time to think, only react. The sound of blade meeting blade rang out in the still night, the mist rising higher, thickening as it came in off the ocean.

Ghostly figures began to form in the mist and the hooded figures started to slash out at them, some of them backing away. The ghostly mist figures broke apart only to reform again.

"What is going on?" one of the hooded figures demanded, backing away from an advancing mist warrior.

"How many have you consigned to the deep?" Kellan continued to fight the leader, driving the man back towards the ocean.

Meikah could only hope the mist figures were something Kellan was doing. After all, rain or mist was his talent. A thick metal chain swung towards her and she dodged out of the way, her lightning arcing between her blade and the chain. It shot along the chain, striking the hooded figure that wielded it, causing him to yelp and drop the chain onto the ground. Hearing movement behind her, she spun in time to block another attack.

Around Meikah some of the hooded figures attacked the mist warriors that rose up around them, enveloping them in their ghostly embrace. One of the hooded figures slashed out with his sword. "They're suffocating me. I feel like I'm trying to breathe under water."

"Maybe you've consigned one too many to the depths," Kellan suggested. "You might want to escape before they drag you out there with them."

"I can't swim." Another one of the hooded figures frantically slashed at the mist warriors with a dagger. "We need to get out of here."

"They're necromancers," another hooded figure stated as she backed away. "Only thing that makes sense. They're raising the dead."

Meikah could have told them that Kellan wasn't raising the dead, only forming figures out of mist, but it was better they thought they were outnumbered. Grinning, she sent her lightning into the weapons of those around her, laughter bubbling up when a few cursed them and one actually dropped their sword.

The only one that wasn't effected by the lightning was a tall man who used a timber staff, striking out with it.

Meikah blocked the staff, the impact shuddering through her arms. Her laughter faded and she focused on trying to avoid being struck by him. Her lightning seemed to have no effect on the tall figure who fought harder when the lightning crackled around the two of them. The ground beneath the one wielding the staff dampened, a puddle slowly forming, barely visible through the mist that continued to swirl around everyone.

"Shade, drive them together," Kellan ordered. "Including the mist warriors. The two of you drop back and remember Suri and Flint's trick." He backed away. The mist becoming heavier.

For a moment Meikah had been about to protest Kellan using Shade's name, then she remembered it wasn't necessary to use their nicknames when they were away from Dreyton. All thoughts of nicknames and worrying about someone figuring out who they were vanished as she realised what Kellan wanted her to do. Shaking her head, she backed away, still trying to avoid being hit by the staff.

The ground beneath her feet dried from the strong wind that picked up, Kellan and Shade moving in close to her. The hooded figures struggled against the wind, water swirling across the ground beneath their feet making it harder for them to stay upright.

"Now, Strike. Hit them," Kellan ordered.

It took her a second to realise he would have used her nickname because people knew she was here. That people knew the two of them were visiting Port Mayren.

"Hurry. Like Suri," Kellan said as rain began to fall on their opponents.

"I might kill them," Meikah protested.

"More are coming. Easily another dozen," Shade said softly.

Meikah glanced around, gaping at the hooded figures coming out from amongst the warehouses towards them. Taking a deep breath, she flung all the lightning she could muster at the rain drenched figures surrounding them, hoping Shade's wind was enough to keep Kellan's rain from them and the lightning from striking them too.

There was a loud crack as the lightning connected with the rain and the air was filled with the scent of burnt hair as their opponents were flung backwards to sprawl across the ground. Lightning played over the ground, forking out in different directions as it died down, the scent of singed hair remaining behind.

The hooded figures that had been moving towards them froze for a moment before running towards their downed companions.

Kellan sheathed his sword and raced forward to grab hold of the hooded figure who'd led the attack, pressing his dagger against the man's throat as he held him tightly. "Back off."

The hooded figures once again froze, the ones lying on the ground, who'd been trying to rise amidst groans, dropped back. Several of them were motionless.

Chapter Fifteen

Meikah wanted to check to see that all of the hooded figures lived. Attacking the living was far different to attacking those who'd already died. "All we need to know is how to get to Durnning Island."

"We don't want any trouble, but we're not about to walk away from it either," Kellan warned.

One of the hooded figures, who'd been approaching, waved the rest of them back. "I'll take you there." She nodded towards the man Kellan held. "Let him go. I'll take you to Durnning Island."

"How can we be certain your word can be trusted?" Shade asked.

The hooded woman drew two daggers, holding them out hilt first. "You can take me prisoner instead."

"Don't listen to her," the man, Kellan held, protested. "She's nothing in our organization."

Kellan grinned. "Yet they all listened to her. Not a single one attacked when she indicated they should fall back." Kellan faced the woman. "What is your name?"

"Jelena." She continued to hold out the daggers hilt first.

Shade sheathed his daggers, coming forward to take the daggers from Jelena. "We accept. When can you take us there?" He remained beside the woman, one of her daggers held near her.

Kellan let go of the man, pushing him away. "Tend to your wounded."

The man shook his head. "I'll take you. Leave her out of it. I'm not about to let her go out there alone with the three of you."

Meikah looked at the two of them, noticing that none of the other hooded figures had come any closer. "You could both come."

"No," Jelena stated. "Neven remains behind."

"If you go, then I do too," Neven argued.

"You will stay here and try to not cause more trouble for me to sort out," Jelena ordered.

Neven took a step towards her. "I don't cause trouble."

Kellan moved between the two of them. "In that case, step away before you do cause more trouble."

Neven looked between Kellan and Jelena. "You're trying to protect her from me?"

Kellan shrugged. "She's unarmed and put herself in our keeping. Now step back."

"I wouldn't attack my sister," Neven protested.

"Some would," Shade said softly.

Wanting to get away from those who'd attacked them in case they decided to try and rescue Jelena and have another go at taking them down, Meikah asked, "Do you have a boat you can use to take us to the island?"

Jelena laughed. "You might say that." She beckoned one of the hooded figures forward. "Ready my boat. None are to remain on board. Any who do will be tossed over the side."

The one she'd beckoned forward nodded before hurrying off.

It didn't take long for the boat to be readied and by the time the hooded figure returned to inform Jelena, she'd arranged for most of the wounded to be collected, regularly telling her brother to stop complaining and that he wasn't going with them, and sent most of her people home. A handful remained, staying well back.

Jelena indicated her daggers Shade continued to

hold. "There's no need to hold them on me. I keep my word."

"I know you do," Shade said.

"Do you know me?" Jelena asked.

"You might say that." Shade smiled briefly.

Dread settled over Meikah. Surely these weren't the children of the dark blade faction leader that Shade had taken out. Worried it was, Meikah spoke before Jelena could reply. "I would like to be back in Port Mayren before daylight."

"This way." Jelena led the way, Shade staying close to her, Neven following. She went further along the coast to where a small sailing boat was anchored just off the shore, a wooden rowboat pulled up on the beach.

Neven went ahead of her, pushing the rowboat into the water, holding it while everyone clambered in before climbing in himself and taking up the oars, ignoring his sister's orders to remain behind.

Meikah smiled at Shade when a warm breeze washed over her legs, drying her boots and trousers that had become soaked when she'd waded into the sea to climb in the boat. Shade gave her a nod before looking towards the sailing boat, continuing to keep the dagger menacingly close to Jelena.

Once they were aboard the sailing boat and the

rowboat was stowed on deck, Jelena drew up the anchor. "If you can put that wind of yours to the sail, we'll reach the island in no time."

Shade remained at her side, nodding as he followed her to the stern of the boat where she stood at the tiller while Neven raised the sail, returning to his sister's side once he was finished.

Meikah sat at the stern of the boat with Kellan, feeling like she was in the way. It wasn't long before they were under way and she stared at the island in the distance, the wind in her face as they raced across the waters towards it. Nearly half an hour passed before they were close enough that she could clearly see the island, jagged rocks scattered through the ocean between them and the land.

She stared at the shore as it came closer and they angled around towards the far side of the island. "We can't land here." The hill rising above the shore and the beach were lined with the dead. A mixture of young, old, male, female, fighters, villagers and everything in between. "We need to turn back."

"You can wait on board," Kellan offered.

She shook her head. "None of us should go ashore. Some of them look like they want revenge."

Neven looked from the shore to Meikah. "You are a necromancer. I wasn't sure, but you must be."

"You're the ones who wanted to come out here," Jelena said. "Are we continuing or turning back?"

"Continue." Kellan faced Meikah. "It's better than the alternative."

Meikah momentarily closed her eyes as she thought of Mezeth. She didn't like any of the options. Her gaze travelled across each of the figures on Durnning Island. "What if they attack?"

"Then we fight." Kellan's hand rested on the hilt of his sword.

"They will have seen what happened here," Shade said. "One of them might be interested in sharing the information with us."

"Nothing was said about us setting foot on Durnning," Neven said. "We'll wait on board for you."

"You expect us to trust you not to leave us behind?" Shade demanded.

"You can remain with them," Kellan said.

Neven laughed. "One against two? You reckon he could take us on and win?"

Meikah wanted to protest. They shouldn't leave Shade with the siblings in case they were his enemies. "I can stay on board."

"You need to go ashore. Mezeth will expect it,"

Kellan said. "Shade can take care of himself. He can always sink the boat if they try anything."

"Then we'd all be stuck here." Jelena turned to Shade. "You can let the wind go now."

Meikah drew in a sharp breath as they sailed close to the jagged rocks the waves crashed against, hoping that whatever the two were using to see in the dark wouldn't wear off. The ship moved into the calmer water past the rocks before Neven dropped the anchor. Her gaze kept returning to the dead who watched them. She dreaded reaching the shore. What if the spirits attacked? There was no way the three of them could face so many of the dead and the other two wouldn't be able to see the spirits. And it'd be even more impossible if one of them remained on board.

Neven nodded towards the shore. "You still want to go over there? I'll lower the rowboat if you do."

Meikah wanted to say 'no'. Wanted to tell them to turn the boat around and head back through the impossibly narrow gaps between the rocks.

"Lower the boat," Kellan said.

"We're not going ashore." Neven readied the rowboat. "Neither of us. No matter what you threaten. There's something wrong with that place.

Gives me the shivers even if I didn't know you can see the dead over there."

Meikah wasn't surprised with the amount of dead that filled the island. "Has anyone ever lived here?"

Jelena shook her head. "It gets hit badly by every storm that comes through the area. Not enough shelter from them."

Kellan turned to Shade. "You sure you're good to stay here?"

Shade inclined his head.

Kellan clapped him on the arm before clambering over the side and into the rowboat, readying the oars. He looked upwards at Meikah. "You coming?"

Chapter Sixteen

After a glance down at Kellan, Meikah again looked at the spirits awaiting her on the island. Several of them had drawn weapons. There was no way they could be back before sunrise. What was Isha going to say when she found her missing?

"We're not staying here all morning," Neven muttered. "We've got better things to do." He rubbed his hand across his arm, glancing towards the island. "Far better things to do."

Meikah climbed over the side and sat at the front of the rowboat on the timber seat. She watched as the island came ever closer. The spirits looked no less menacing the closer they came to them. If anything, they looked more threatening with their narrowed eyes and hard set jaws. She rested her hand on the hilt of her sword. She doubted they'd let them on their island without a fight.

One of the warriors came to the edge of the water. "The living aren't welcome here."

"We don't plan on staying long." Kellan kept rowing.

A second warrior came to stand beside the first, a greatsword held ready. "This is our island. The last thing we want here are the living."

Kellan remained in the shallows. "We don't plan to stay long."

"You're not staying at all," the first warrior warned.

"There's a cave-"

The first warrior interrupted Kellan. "Last warning. Turn around."

"We can't do that." Kellan dipped the oars in the water.

More warriors joined the first one, all with their weapons drawn.

"If you can tell us what happened to the dragon who was in the cave, we won't have to come onto your island." Meikah wasn't sure if she should draw her weapons. Considering how outnumbered they were, drawing them was likely to cause more problems than it solved.

A child pushed through the crowd. "Why would we tell you anything?"

Meikah had no answer for him. It wasn't like they

could bribe them. What did the dead need other than to be left in peace? "What would it hurt you to tell us what we need to know?"

One of the men at the water's edge stood with his hands on his hips, seeming to have no weapons. "What have the living ever done for us other than to kill us or forget our existence?"

Kellan climbed out of the boat, tugging it towards the shore. One of the warriors stepped in front of him. Kellan's hand rested on his dagger, the other remaining on the boat. "You don't want this to become a fight."

"You think you know what we want?" the weaponless man demanded.

Meikah clambered out of the boat as the hull scraped against the sand, still not drawing her weapons. She was pretty sure that the moment one of them drew a weapon the dead would attack.

"Does anyone truly know what another wants?" Kellan asked.

"Why are we standing around here talking?" the child demanded. "They've already had their last warning."

Meikah eyed the distance between her and the land, the spirits blocking her view. "Was the dragon dead when he was taken from the island?"

"What's it got to do with you?" the child demanded. Several of the spirits murmured in agreement.

"Why aren't we doing something about them?" one of the men asked.

"They don't normally talk back to us," another one said.

"Who sits on the throne?" the weaponless man asked.

"King Branok," Meikah said. "The son."

"How is that meant to help?" the first warrior demanded. "Could have had a dozen kings by that name for all we know."

"He's our second king by that name," Meikah said.

Kellan tried to push the boat onto the shore since the spirits remained in his way, making it impossible for him to drag it onto the sand. None of them moved, continuing to block his efforts.

"I've had enough of this." The child drew out a dagger, throwing himself at Meikah.

She automatically drew her weapons, lightning racing along the blades as she blocked his attack, moving towards the shore. She didn't want to remain knee deep in the water in case her magic should get out of control.

The child stumbled back, his gaze fixed on the blades. "Necromancer."

A few others backed away, murmuring amongst themselves.

"What did you think we were?" Kellan finally managed to push the rowboat onto the sandy beach.

"Not all who can see us have the ability to fight us," the first warrior said.

The child backed further away, tugging on the arm of one of the warriors. "We get killed by them, we'll be dead and gone."

"I'm not about to stay here for them to end my existence." One of the warriors, that hadn't drawn a weapon, retreated.

The weaponless man raised his fists, stalking towards Meikah. "That suits me fine. You can't call this much of an existence anyway. It'll be a relief to have an end to it." He swung at Meikah. "If they're capable."

Meikah jumped out of the way, trying to angle towards the shore. Other spirits got in her way and she tried to avoid colliding with them. Several joined the weaponless man while a handful of warriors attacked Kellan.

"You're crazy." The child had backed well away

from the shore. "Tell them what they want to know so we can get rid of them."

Meikah splashed through the ocean, blocking and weaving to avoid the attackers. When a fist passed her defences, she stumbled back, reeling from the impact. Pain radiated through her and she barely managed to block the spirit's next attack. "We just need to know who took the dragon and if he was dead or alive."

"Doubt it'd be dead with the amount of chains they wrapped-" The child broke off abruptly.

Meikah glanced towards him to find he struggled against two spirits, one with a hand clamped over his mouth. "Why can't you tell us the information?"

"Why should we help you?" the weaponless man demanded.

Meikah couldn't come up with a single reason that would make sense to the dead.

"We could take a message to the living." Kellan fought the spirits surrounding him, his sword connecting with their weapons.

"Do you have any unfinished business?" Meikah pressed forward, not sure what she'd do if more joined the attack. She was barely remaining on her feet, the weaponless man surprisingly quick considering how large he was.

The weaponless man laughed mirthlessly. "Would

you carry a dagger to someone for me and deliver it between their ribs?"

"None of those who died or are buried here went peacefully," a woman warned. "Revenge is the main unfinished business we all have in common."

Chapter Seventeen

Meikah finally stumbled onto the shore. It didn't help. A blow knocked her to the ground and her sword fell from her hand. She raised her hand as if to block the weaponless man. The lacey dragon burst forth, knocking him from his feet, causing the few who closed in on her to stumble backwards.

He staggered to his feet, staring at Meikah who also rose to her feet. "What are you?" he demanded.

"Necromancer and dragon touched." She warily watched him, wishing her sword was within easy reach. But she didn't dare take her gaze off him so moving was certainly out of the question.

"We're never magic users. Always warriors."

Meikah opened her mouth to speak, but no words came out. She stared at him, eventually trying to speak again. "We?"

"What do they teach you these days?" He

demanded. "Once I would have been able to recognise what you are from a distance. Back when I lived."

Meikah wanted to collect her sword, but didn't dare move. Not while everyone remained still and no one attacked her or Kellan. "I've been taught nothing." At least she hadn't been taught anything about being dragon touched. She was still learning what it meant to be a necromancer.

"What do you mean you've been taught nothing?" He demanded. "Has our organization deteriorated that much over the past century?"

Meikah shrugged. "I don't think there is an organization anymore. Or at least Mezeth didn't think there were any other dragon touched left."

He came closer to her. "You've spoken to her? She knows who you are?"

"She sent me here." Meikah forced herself to remain where she was and not retreat from the man who loomed over her.

"Why didn't you tell me sooner?"

She nearly demanded how she was meant to have known that it would have made a difference.

"None of this has anything to do with us. The matters of the living are none of our concern," one of the warriors, who'd also attacked Meikah, said.

The weaponless man glared at the other warrior. "It might not be your business, but it is mine."

His words caused an argument to start amongst the spirits, some of them coming to blows while the rest yelled over the top of each other. Threats were traded, along with insults, and the noise rose.

Meikah moved an inch at a time towards her sword. Not that the spirits seemed to pay any attention to her. She was about to pick it up when one of the spirits spoke.

"Why don't we have the necromancers take us to the shore?" Her words brought silence.

Meikah grabbed her sword. She wasn't about to take the spirits to the mainland. Not vengeful spirits. "You've already told us that all any of you are interested in is vengeance."

"All those I would avenge myself against should be dead by now," one of the warriors said. "I just want to see my home one last time."

"The one I would have revenge against is a necromancer," the weaponless man said. "They never die. But I can make his existence an eternal misery."

"Didn't you say it's been a century?" Meikah asked.

"Do you think I should let Amiel get away with all he's done to me no matter the amount of time that's passed?"

Shock arrowed through Meikah, causing her to take half a step back before she halted her movements.

He grabbed her by the shoulders, gripping her tightly. "You know him?"

She slowly shook her head. It couldn't be possible. "The name isn't uncommon."

"You know a necromancer by that name."

She met his angry gaze, wanting to deny his words. The hate and anger in his eyes were almost tangible. "I can't help you." His grip on her shoulders became painful. "Let me go."

"What if we offer to take four of you to the mainland?" Kellan asked. "Only those of you not focused on vengeance."

"I will tell you everything you need to know if you would take me to the mainland and lead me to Amiel," the weaponless man promised.

She tried to draw away from his grip, but it was impossible. "I can't help you." She wanted to ask what Amiel had done to him, but feared it would convince her that helping him was the right thing to do. Around them other spirits argued about why they should be taken to the mainland. She wanted to demand why nothing was ever simple.

He shook her as the arguing around them became

louder, fights breaking out again. "You want information. I do too."

She felt the air crackle around her as her magic rose. "Last warning. Let me go." She might be too close to him to do major damage, but hopefully what she could do would be enough to make him release his hold on her.

"You ask him how many dragon touched he's killed. Ask him how long it will be before he kills you for being dragon touched."

Again she found herself wanting to protest, but the words died before they formed at the look she saw in his eyes. A shudder ran through her. "He can't harm me." Her words were soft and filled with the uncertainty she felt. Surely whatever he had against dragon touched was unimportant compared to the deal he'd made with Danton.

"He can't be trusted. He'd stab you in the back the moment there was the slightest benefit in it for him."

"I know."

His grip loosened on her shoulders. "You know?"

"I don't trust the Amiel I know." She was finally able to wrench herself from his grip and take a step back. "That doesn't mean he's the same Amiel you've sworn vengeance against."

Kellan shouldered his way through the spirits.

"What if we exchange information with you? I'll show you what the Amiel we know looks like if you tell us who took the dragon."

"Don't do it Daveth," one of the warriors ordered. "You'd give up our only means of bargaining for something so pathetic?"

"You're all crazy," the woman said. "The only thing keeping us in existence is this island. Set foot on the mainland, and you'll cease to exist." Her words brought more arguments.

"Anyone want to test that theory?" Kellan grinned. "I'll take one of you to the mainland."

"I'm more than willing to test it," Daveth said.

Meikah found herself wanting to protest. From Kellan's tone, she assumed he thought the woman correct. She turned to Daveth. "Why would you be willing to do that?"

Daveth made a sweeping gesture that encompassed the island and arguing spirits. "You think this is much of an existence?"

"I'm sorry."

Before Meikah could stop him, Daveth had pulled off her mask. He let her take the item from him. "You're younger than I thought. What are the dragons thinking letting one so young and with no training to fend for themselves?"

"Letha made me dragon touched."

"I don't know that name. But ones without power amongst dragons shouldn't be creating dragon touched where they please," Daveth stated.

Kellan glanced towards the sailing boat. "We can't stay here all day. The sun will rise soon and the dark blades will be getting impatient."

"Do you know if they're…" Meikah's voice trailed off as she looked between Daveth and the sailing boat. She didn't want to give the spirits any information about Shade and his possible enemies.

Kellan nodded. "Which is why I don't want to leave them together any longer than necessary."

Chapter Eighteen

Meikah sheathed her weapons before putting her mask back on. She met Daveth's gaze. "I won't take you to the mainland if all that awaits you is your spirit can no longer remain in this world. I won't be responsible for your complete death." It seemed wrong since he was dragon touched like her. Someone who'd been willing to protect dragons.

Daveth tilted his head slightly, studying her. "Do others know you're a necromancer?"

"Not many," Meikah said.

Daveth inclined his head. "That explains it. Give it time. You'll become bitter and disillusioned the more who know what you are."

"Are you willing to exchange information with us?" Kellan asked Daveth.

"The image of the Amiel you know in exchange for who took Galzeren." Daveth held out his hand.

Before Kellan could take his hand, a warrior barrelled into them, striking out at Daveth with his sword. Kellan threw himself at the warrior, tackling him to the ground and driving his dagger into his side. The spirit threw Kellan back before he could attack again.

Daveth joined the fight, fists rapidly pummelling the warrior. "You will not interfere."

"You're not the only one stuck here." The warrior warily circled Daveth.

Before the warrior could reach him, Kellan stepped in front of Daveth, his hand out. The moment Daveth took his hand, he said, "Deal." A figure formed beside him out of mist as the warrior hollered and threw himself at the mist figure that broke apart only to reform.

Daveth pointed at the misty figure. "That's him. That's the one who caused my death along with several others. We were visiting Port Mayren. They slaughtered the lot of us and dumped our bodies here."

"The battle out here lasted for days," a warrior said, a sword in each of her hands. "We were raised over and over again."

Meikah frowned. "What battle?"

The warrior shrugged, making a sweeping gesture

towards the spirits around her. "Think they would have told us anything?"

"What battle are you talking about?" Kellan let the mist figure disperse. "How long ago was it?"

"Timell was on the throne," Daveth said. "He'd only been king for a few years."

"A century ago?" Meikah asked.

Daveth shrugged, as did the warrior who shared a look with Daveth. She faced Meikah again. "There was unrest in the city. A new king, the unexpected death of the old one and fighting amongst many of the factions. Everyone wanted power. But don't they always? We came down out of the Arcton Mountains and stepped into a mess. The dragons wanted to know what was going on amongst humans. They'd heard rumours. Three of us went to find out. None of us returned."

"Whatever battle it was, it's probably long since over," Kellan said.

Daveth nodded. "I owe you information. It was sorcerers who took Galzeren. At least a dozen of them arrived on the island, using magic to lift him out of the cave and transport him to the ship that awaited them beyond the rocks."

"What was the name of the ship?" Meikah asked.

"I'll tell you that information if you take me to the mainland," Daveth said.

"No," the warrior protested. "Don't leave here, Daveth. We'll never learn exactly what happened if you do that."

Daveth rested a hand on the warrior's shoulder. "We won't learn what happened if we stay here, Marta. Our only chance of revenge and hearing the full truth is by escaping this imprisonment."

"Death is not an escape. It's an end," Marta said.

"The necromancers could prevent that from happening." Daveth nodded towards them.

"Even if I knew how to do it, why would I when you want to go after Amiel?" Meikah asked.

"He's your friend?" Marta asked.

Meikah shook her head as she tried to come up with an explanation. "He's my teacher."

"I think you need a new one," Daveth said dryly. "Especially since you don't know how to raise the dead or keep them in existence."

Meikah held his gaze a moment before she replied. "I choose not to raise the dead." She didn't want to become a necromancer. It was bad enough she had the power to become one and was considered one.

"That doesn't mean you can't prevent the dead from fading from this world," Daveth said.

Meikah was tempted to ask him what he meant, but wasn't sure she wanted to have anything to do with keeping spirits in this world, no matter the means used.

"Don't risk it," Marta pleaded with Daveth. "One day the right person will find their way to this island and we'll return home as well as discover what happened in Port Mayren."

Marta's tone made Meikah feel guilty for refusing to help. The warrior sounded desperate. "I can't help you." She wished she could tell them something different. But helping someone who planned to go after Amiel was a terrible idea.

Some of the spirits drifted away, the majority of the warriors remaining behind. The first warrior who'd spoken stepped between Marta and Daveth. "You would desert us? After all these decades, you'd leave like this."

Daveth raised an eyebrow. "You expect me to believe you'd wait?"

The warrior glanced away, unable to look Daveth in the eye. "I'd find a way for everyone to get off this forsaken island."

Kellan grinned. "Even I can tell that's a lie." He turned to Daveth. "What if I try to find out what war occurred during the early years of Timell's reign and bring news back to you? Would you tell us the name of the ship then?"

"How can I trust you to return?" Daveth asked. "Take me with you."

Marta pointed out to sea. "Looks like a fight broke out on the sailing boat."

Meikah spun to see Shade dive overboard and swim towards the shore. Jelena dragged Neven back from the side of the sailing boat when he would have followed. Neven yelled after Shade, his words torn away by the wind, only the angry tone reaching them on the island. Meikah watched Shade swim towards them through the calm waters between the ship and the rocks.

Reaching the shore, Shade waded out to join them, glancing at the spirits. "They know who I am."

"How did they figure that out?" Kellan met Shade at the water's edge. "You escaped without injury?"

Marta spoke before Shade had the chance to do little more than nod. "Looks like you're stuck here too."

Meikah stared at the boat that was sailing through the gaps between the rocks, the grey of the coming dawn beginning to fill the sky. "My grandmother will be so worried."

"You should be more concerned about yourself," Daveth said.

"People will come looking for us," Kellan said. "There are others who know we planned to come here."

Meikah continued to watch the ship until it rounded the island and slipped out of sight. "I only hope it's people and not a dragon who comes looking for us." She dreaded to think what devastation Mezeth would cause to Port Mayren and the surrounding areas.

"Which dragon?" Marta asked.

"Mezeth," Meikah said.

Marta smiled wistfully. "I'd love to talk to her again. To have form enough that she could see and hear me." Her smile faded. "I tried. The few times she returned here. I tried."

Shade glanced at the warriors that remained on the shore. "Did you learn anything?"

"Sorcerers took him." Kellan turned his back on the ocean. "We should have a look in the cave."

One of the warriors grinned. "Going to check out your new home?"

Another warrior chuckled. "For all your threats and demands you're as stuck here as the rest of us."

Most of the warriors wandered away, making jokes

at their expense, only Daveth and Marta staying behind. Daveth waited until they were alone before he spoke. "None of you are concerned about being stranded here."

Chapter Nineteen

Meikah looked at each of her companions, not sure what she should say. Would it be best if the two dead dragon touched thought the same as the rest of the warriors? "I already told you. Someone will come for us."

"Where is the cave?" Kellan asked.

"You expect us to help you when you offer nothing in return?" Daveth demanded.

"The island isn't that big." Kellan scanned the area. "And we'll have more than enough time to find it before someone comes looking for us."

Marta sighed. "This way."

Daveth hurried after her. "What are you doing?"

"This isn't us. We aren't the sort to make demands and force people to do our bidding. We spent our lives keeping peace between dragons and humans. Death shouldn't change who we are." Marta led the way to a tumble of boulders. There was a large cave opening beyond them.

Vines and shrubs had been torn away to make it easier to access the cave and there were gouges in the dirt at the entrance and deep claw marks on the walls like some creature had fought to remain. Meikah ran a finger across the marks in the wall. "What happened?"

"And when did it happen?" Kellan asked.

"Smugglers found the cave," Marta said. "They'd planned to leave crates of stolen goods here, but discovered the dragon instead. One of them said he knew someone who'd pay good money for news of him." She fell silent a moment. "We could do nothing. They came, a few weeks back, at least a dozen of them, casting their spells and chaining him like a beast. He woke from his hibernation, his wound nearly healed, chained and captured. He wasn't strong enough to escape from them. He tried, but he'd been too long in hibernation."

Daveth rested a hand on Marta's shoulder. "We have nothing to feel guilty about. We're spirits. How could we have done much against them?"

Marta shrugged his hand from her shoulder. "Which is why we should help the necromancers. They can do something."

"How can we trust them?" Daveth asked.

"She's dragon touched. How can we not trust her?" Marta gestured sharply towards Meikah.

"But did she become dragon touched before or after she was a necromancer?" Daveth asked.

Marta remained silent, turning away from all of them to step outside of the cave, her shoulders slumped.

Meikah hurried after her. "I don't see how it matters, but I became dragon touched after I learned I was-" She broke off, not wanting to say she was a necromancer. "After I learned I could see the dead."

Marta studied her. "You don't want to be a necromancer."

Meikah shook her head.

"I'm sorry." Marta smiled briefly, one tinged with sorrow. "I would have given anything to have been a necromancer after the years I've spent here. I was born to serve dragons. It's all I've ever wanted to do. Instead, I'm bound to this island and forced to watch as dragons are captured and dragged away to who knows what fate."

"I can't help you," Meikah said softly.

Marta smiled again, the same sorrow tinged smile as before. "You could. I just don't think you know how. Just like I don't think you know how to be dragon touched. We could teach you."

Shock raced through Meikah. It took all her willpower not to leap at the chance. "Amiel can't be killed."

"I know. You can't kill a necromancer," Marta said. "Or at least not in a way to wipe one out of existence."

Daveth joined them. "You can make their life, and death, miserable."

Meikah faced him. "Even if I knew how to help the two of you, do you think I would when you make comments like that?"

Shade smiled. "It's comments like that which tempts me to help them."

Kellan chuckled. "Same here." His amusement faded. "Except it'd cause problems for Mace and Danton. I wouldn't want that for either of them."

"What if we waited until neither of them lived?" Daveth asked. "I've waited this long for justice, I can wait longer if I know it's within my reach."

"They're necromancers," Shade said.

"Justice!" Marta faced Daveth. "It's revenge."

Daveth shrugged. "Sometimes they're the same thing."

"What do you want?" Kellan asked Marta.

"Knowledge. I want to know what happened and why it happened. I want to know why we were forced to fight over and over again for seemingly no reason only to be left here for decades."

"We'll return with whatever knowledge we learn," Kellan promised.

Marta inclined her head. "Thank you."

Shade turned to Daveth. "How many sorcerers died?"

"Three."

Meikah glanced over her shoulder at the cave. "How do you know they died?"

Shade led the way, pointing out large, rust-coloured stains on the ground. There was also a broken sword and a shattered staff. "Even weakened, Galzeren was a formidable opponent."

"Yes. The perfect mate for Mezeth. Her equal," Marta said. "He must be found. There are so few ancestors left." She sighed. "Or at least there were a century ago. I have no idea what things are currently like."

Meikah stared at the rusty marks. It was better than seeing the pain and sorrow in Marta's eyes. "We need to know the name of the ship that took him."

"It was The Lucky Spark," Marta said.

Daveth opened his mouth to speak, but closed it

instead with a shake of his head before he strode away.

Marta stared after him. "It's worse for him. He was the one who talked me into going. I'd always wanted to see the capital, but every time I had the chance, the dragons needed me." A wry smile formed. "I guess he was right when he said I'd best visit while I had the chance because life was too short to keep putting things off." She took a step in the direction Daveth had taken. "I should go talk to him." She started for the entrance, pausing to speak over her shoulder. "Whoever organised Galzeren's capture remained on board. One of them kept saying not to harm the dragon any more than necessary or they'd be the one to answer as to why it was harmed when they got him back to the ship."

Shade waited until they were alone before he spoke, keeping his voice low. "We can use the rowboat and I can use the winds to help us return to Port Mayren."

"I can keep the waters around us calm," Kellan offered.

"I doubt you'd want my ability to help us return to the capital," Meikah said.

Kellan grinned. "You can help if there's a welcoming party for us at the harbour."

"We can land where it's busy. No one would try anything then." Shade glanced towards the cave entrance, stepping closer to Kellan and Meikah. "That name Marta gave us, it's the name of the ship belonging to the King."

Meikah's mouth dropped open slightly as she struggled to make sense of everything. "He knows? He sent us out here when he already knows?"

Kellan frowned. "That doesn't make sense. Why the sorcerers? If it was the King, he'd send soldiers."

"He might have sent sorcerers because he knew how difficult it would be to get Galzeren out to the ship," Shade suggested.

"Then why would he send for me?" Meikah asked.

"To track down all those who know the truth," Shade suggested.

"How are we meant to-" Meikah broke off. "Oh."

"What?" Kellan and Shade spoke at the same time.

"Your uncle was complaining about the prince spending time with the daughter of the Sorcerer Academy's director."

Kellan slowly nodded. "So is the King and the director in on this together or is the daughter using the prince to gain access to the ship?"

"Or the director could be using the prince's

infatuation with his daughter to gain access to the ship," Shade suggested.

Meikah groaned. "This is getting too complicated. How are we meant to figure all of this out? Who can we trust?"

"Not a sorcerer," Shade said. "Power at all cost. They live by their code."

Chapter Twenty

Meikah drew in a sharp breath. Surely it couldn't be the director. But that was no worse than it being the King. "No one would believe us. Why would the director risk his position to do something so illegal?"

"Power," Kellan said. "There are many powerful potions and spells that can be created with dragon parts."

"You think Galzeren's dead?" Meikah's gaze was drawn to the claw marks gouged into the walls of the cave. It didn't seem fair they'd gone after him while he'd been vulnerable. Even in his weakened state he'd fought so hard.

"That depends on what parts of him they're using," Kellan said.

"So he could be alive?" Meikah held her breath until Kellan nodded, relief rushing through her as she breathed out. "We need to find him while there's a chance he lives."

"The director of the Sorcerer Academy has a place outside of Port Mayren, further along the coast. He calls it a manor house, but it's large enough and has enough fortifications it might as well be a castle," Shade said.

Meikah stared at him. "You want us to break into what is basically a castle? One filled with sorcerers." She wished they could tell the King, but there was a chance it could be him who'd arranged to have the dragon captured. She frowned. Yet why would he capture one to use for spells and potions and send for the dragon touched to help another? He had his soldiers if Shade's theory was correct. If he wanted to learn who knew he'd taken Galzeren, he could have sent his soldiers. "This doesn't make sense. It can't be the King. He wants us to help Mezeth. Surely we could go to him and tell him everything we've learned."

"As I said earlier, there are places his soldiers can't go. But, even if he is innocent, we'd need strong proof," Kellan said. "He wouldn't want to make an enemy of an entire faction."

Dread settled over Meikah. "What if Galzeren isn't there? What if he's keeping him somewhere else?

What if for some crazy reason it is the King? What then?"

"What if this is the King's way to get the director out of the way and put his own director in place?" Shade asked.

Silence filled the cave and Meikah wanted to beg Shade to take back his words. "How are we meant to figure any of this out? We don't have the experience to deal with this."

"You might not have, but I was raised on intrigue," Shade said.

"Then what do we do?" Meikah asked.

"We take it one step at a time. First, we get off this island and then we find out who last used The Lucky Spark," Shade said.

"Then what?" Meikah asked.

Shade shrugged. "We see what we learn and figure out what to do next." He glanced in the direction of the entrance. "I know how to keep the spirits bound to this world."

Meikah took a step back from him. "They'd go after Amiel."

"Marta wouldn't. She only wants answers," Kellan said.

After all they'd learned, she wasn't sure if she'd ever be able to believe what anyone told her. She wasn't sure she could deal with intrigue on a regular basis. "Does she? We only have her word for it. At least with Daveth we know he wants revenge. He isn't keeping any secrets about his intentions."

Kellan captured Meikah's hand, holding it tightly. "Don't let any of this change you. There are good people in this world." He grinned. "And good spirits."

She sighed heavily. "I don't know what to believe."

"We can always come back. Nothing has to be decided today," Shade said.

Some of the dread shifted and Meikah sent him a grateful smile. "Good. I think we've got enough to focus on." Another thought occurred to her and her smile widened. "We can ask Mezeth about them. She'll know what they're like."

"What they used to be like," Shade warned.

Meikah's smile vanished. "Oh."

Kellan chuckled. "Quit worrying. We better get back before Isha goes asking questions and notifying the wrong people of our disappearance."

Meikah tugged her hand from Kellan's. "Why are we still standing around here?" She strode towards the entrance.

Kellan hurried after her, slowing when he reached her side. "We weren't standing around. We were making plans."

Shade walked at Meikah's other side. "Kellan's favourite pastime."

Meikah managed a smile, but it faded almost before it finished forming. There were so many things they didn't know and it seemed like things were becoming more complicated the more they learned. How bad would things be by the end of the day once they'd learned more information?

Daveth waited for them by the rowboat. No one else was in sight. "I wanted to apologise."

"For what?" Kellan asked.

"I let my wants get in the way of my beliefs. I should have told you everything I knew about Galzeren instead of using the information as a way to escape this place," Daveth said.

Meikah wanted to believe him. But after everything she'd learned, she still had no idea who to trust. "We will try to save him."

Daveth nodded. "As you should." He paused a moment. "Can I ask a favour of you?" A wry smile made a brief appearance. "It has nothing to do with Amiel. I would ask only that you carry a message to Mezeth for me."

"That depends on what the message is." Meikah hated how suspicious she felt.

"Tell her Galzeren fought bravely. Even weakened

from hibernation, he didn't go quietly and took the lives of three of his enemies. We were unable to do little more in our spirit state other than witness his ferocity and bravery."

Meikah smiled, relief rushing through her. "Yes. I can tell her that."

Daveth held out his hand to her. "Thank you."

Meikah shook his hand. It felt as solid as hers. It was hard to believe that to most other people it was like he didn't exist.

"If you have the need of a trainer, you know where I am." He continued to hold her hand, a wry smile making a brief appearance. "It's not like I can go anywhere else."

"I can't-"

Daveth interrupted Meikah. "No strings. You can stay here and I'll teach you what it means to be dragon touched." He finally let go of her hand. "That was one of my tasks. Training those new to our faction." His jaw hardened. "I trained both those I led to their death. I'll never forgive Amiel for that, but I shouldn't blame you for his actions even though I can't understand how you could be his friend."

"I'm not his friend," Meikah said.

"His student then," Daveth said.

She tried to think of how to explain the situation.

"It's complicated, but being trained by him is preferable to accidentally killing someone I care for."

Daveth remained silent for a moment. "I can understand a noble choice like that." He bowed to her. "Again I apologise for not finding out the details of the situation and making assumptions instead." He stepped to the side. "I kept the other spirits from damaging your vessel in case you needed it to make your way out to the ship that comes to rescue you. There were a few willing to use up all their energy and lose what little claim they have on this existence in an effort to make it impossible for you to leave."

"Thanks." Kellan pushed the rowboat into the water. "We're going to return to Port Mayren in it."

"Are you crazy?" Daveth demanded.

Kellan grinned. "More than likely. But between us we should have the necessary skills to reach the harbour."

Daveth rested his hand on Meikah's shoulder. "Good luck."

"Thank you." She met his gaze a moment longer before she waded out to the rowboat Kellan held and clambered in.

Once Shade climbed in, Kellan pushed the rowboat further out before joining them, grabbing the oars. A breeze picked up behind them and the gentle waves flattened out in front of them.

Chapter Twenty-One

Meikah nodded towards the oars Kellan used. "Did you want me to row since you're both busy?"

Kellan swapped places with her and handed over the oars. "That'd be good."

She dipped the oar into the water, surprised at how much resistance there was. "Is it meant to be so hard to row?"

"That'll be what I'm doing to the waves," Kellan said. "They might have been calm close to the shore, but they're getting rougher the closer we come to the rocks."

She studied him, surprised at the amount of strain in his voice. "What's wrong?"

His grin was strained. "You try fighting the ocean."

"Oh." She forced the oar through the water. "Is there anything else I can do to help?"

"Keep the boat on coarse." Kellan pointed to a narrow gap between two rocks. "Aim for that point."

Meikah forced the oars through the water, the wind at her back, waves rising up from on either side of the glassy path Kellan created. Spray struck her when some of the waves tried to crash down on them, torn apart by gusts of wind. The closer they came to the rocks, the harder it was to keep the rowboat heading in the correct direction. "It's like it wants to go straight into the rocks."

"I can't calm the ocean down enough to stop it from pushing against the boat." Kellan gripped the side of the rowboat as he peered over it, his knuckles white. "I can't hold the ocean much longer. Can you row faster?"

Meikah again forced the oar through the water. It didn't go any faster than it already was. "This is as fast as I can go." The rowboat began to shudder and shiver, going off course bit by bit. She stared at the approaching rock. They were going to hit it.

"Should I reduce the amount of wind?" Shade asked.

"It won't help," Kellan said. "If we take too long, I won't be able to hold the waves back."

Meikah struggled to force the oar into the water. It was impossible. The rowboat continued to go off course and she was unable to turn it. The rocks loomed ahead of them. "This isn't working."

"What if you use the waves to lift us over the rocks?" Shade suggested.

"I don't have that much control over them." Kellan continued to grip the side of the rowboat, his tone filled with the strain.

The rock was inches away. Meikah leapt to her feet and dashed to the front of the rowboat as she dropped one of the oars into the bottom of it. She jabbed at the rock with the oar she clutched in both hands, jabbing it a second time. The rowboat scraped along the rock, splinters torn from it. She forced it away from the rock with another jab from the oar, spinning to face the rock on the other side as they drew near to it. She pushed the boat away, not using as much force this time. Then they were past the rocks and she started to sink down onto the seat. Movement on the ocean caught her attention. She stared at the numerous sailing ships heading towards them.

"That could be a problem." Shade nodded towards the oncoming ships. "Looks like Jelena and Neven plan to keep their promise."

Meikah sat down heavily as she counted the oncoming ships. "How are we meant to face five of them?"

"We can't," Kellan said. "Stow the oars in the bottom of the boat and hang on."

"What are you going to do?" Meikah pushed the oars under the seats.

"Create a channel of fast flowing water." Kellan glanced at Shade. "Can you take the wind from their sails?"

Shade nodded, the surrounding breeze dying down.

"Is there anything I can do?" Meikah looked from the approaching ships to the harbour and back again.

Kellan grinned. "Hold on."

She'd barely managed to hold on when the rowboat shot forward, jarring as it skipped across the waves. The distance between them and the ships increased and they soon left them well behind. The rowboat slowed as they approached a dock. "Should Shade return to Dreyton rather than risk being caught by Jelena and Neven?"

"I won't leave you to face all of this on your own." Shade looked over his shoulder towards the ships that had changed direction to keep following them. "I didn't think they'd recognise me. Not after all this time. I'm sorry it caused problems for you."

Kellan grabbed a rope hanging from the side of the dock and tied the rowboat to it. "We'll manage."

He climbed out, stumbling as he reached the dock. He waited until they were all on the dock before he spoke again. "We better go back to my uncle's and make sure no one has sent for the guards to look for us."

"I'll let the King know we've returned and ask around about when The Lucky Spark was last taken out and who took it out," Shade said.

Kellan grinned. "Don't get caught."

With a nod and a smile, Shade strode along the dock.

Meikah was surprised by how comforting she found the familiar words Kellan had spoken. "I hope Grandmother Isha hasn't notified anyone."

Kellan slung an arm around her shoulders, his pace slower than usual as they walked along the dock. "We'll sort it out if she has."

Meikah studied him. "Are you all right?"

"We'll be at my uncle's soon and can rest."

They remained silent during the walk back to Garven's house. Meikah's steps slowed further as they drew near, exhaustion and tiredness tugging at her. She hated to think how exhausted Kellan must feel. "I can't see anyone."

"Then we better climb onto the roof and in our windows before they do send for someone." Kellan headed towards the side of the house where it was easiest to climb onto the roof.

Meikah made her way to the window of the room she was staying in. She was halfway inside when she realised Isha was in the corner, watching her. She froze, not sure what to do or how to explain what she was wearing.

"I guess you can't tell me the reason you're dressed like the ones the Duke sent with us and what you've been doing all night," Isha said.

Meikah finished climbing in the window. "Sorry."

"Can you at least leave a letter in future letting me know who to contact if you don't return? Someone who can go after you if you end up in more trouble than you can handle." Isha crossed the room to stand in front of Meikah.

"Someone knew where I was." Meikah removed her mask, feeling odd to wear it in front of Isha.

"I'm glad." Smiling, Isha wrapped her arms around Meikah. "If you need anything, you come to me. I'll help you without question."

Meikah returned Isha's hug, eventually drawing back. "Thank you."

"I trust you, Meikie. You've a good heart." Isha started for the door, glancing over her shoulder as she reached it. "Are you hungry?"

"No, I just want to sleep."

Isha smiled. "Then sleep. I'll see that no one disturbs you."

"Thank you." Meikah stared at the closed door, reeling from the conversation. She was still staring at the door when there was a light tap on it before it opened.

Kellan stepped inside, closing the door behind him, no longer wearing his travel outfit. "I saw Isha leaving your room."

Meikah nodded.

"What did you tell her?"

"Nothing."

"How did you manage that?"

Meikah slowly shook her head, still trying to figure everything out. "She didn't want to know anything. Just asked that I leave a letter with her of who she can contact if things go wrong and I don't come home."

"She's had experience with this before?"

"My grandfather. These days he might be a diplomat, but when he was younger, he used to go on secret missions for the Duke. No one ever really spoke of it, but we all knew he did something dangerous."

Kellan glanced over his shoulder. "We should both get some sleep. As soon as Shade learns anything useful, we'll probably have to make plans for what to do next."

"All right."

"Unless you have a better offer than sleep." Kellan grinned.

Meikah couldn't resist returning his grin. "All I want to do is sleep. And I'm sure you do too."

Kellan pressed a hand to his heart. "That was a painful blow."

Meikah crossed the room and held open the door. "Good night. Or good morning. I'm not sure which suits."

Kellan moved close to her, resting a hand on her hip. "How about pleasant dreams?"

She met his gaze, breathing in sharply when she saw his expression. "Pleasant dreams." The words came out softer than she expected.

Kellan leaned in close, his lips a mere breath from hers. "I will." With a smile he stepped away and strode to his room.

Chapter Twenty-Two

Closing the door, Meikah sagged against it, surprised at how fast her heart beat. She remained against the door, eyes closed as she replayed the moment. All it would have taken was for her to have leaned in the slightest and her lips would have met Kellan's. Pushing away from the door, she frowned, trying to figure out if she was disappointed or relieved. Was it possible to be both?

Not coming to any conclusion, she readied herself for bed, falling instantly asleep the moment she lay down. It was late afternoon when she was woken by a hand on her shoulder.

Shade stood beside her bed, drawing back when her eyes opened. "When you're ready, I'll meet you in Kellan's room."

She nodded, waiting until he left the room before she stumbled out of bed, rubbing sleep from her eyes.

It felt like she could have easily slept a few more hours. Once she'd dressed for the day, she headed to Kellan's room, knocking lightly on the door before she entered.

Kellan sat in the middle of his bed, a plate of food on his lap. He pointed to another plate on a chest of drawers. "Isha said there's more if we're still hungry."

Meikah picked up the plate, looking for somewhere to sit.

Grinning, Kellan shifted over on the bed, patting the mattress. "Plenty of room."

She sat on the end of the bed, looking up at Shade who remained by the window, standing to the side of it as he stared outside. "What did you learn?"

"The prince is an imbecile and all we can hope is that he dies from misadventure before he has the chance to inherit the throne." Shade faced the room, remaining by the window.

Meikah stared at him, her food halfway to her mouth. "That's treason."

"Treason would be making certain he found that misadventure," Shade said.

"What did he do?" Kellan asked.

"The director's daughter talked him into taking her sailing. Seems he ended up seasick and spent the entire time in his cabin, adamant it was something he ate since he'd never been seasick before in his life," Shade said.

Meikah swallowed her mouthful. "She gave him something to make him sick?"

Shade shrugged. "That's the logical assumption."

"The question is, was she working alone or with her father?" Kellan set aside his empty plate and rose to his feet. "We need to visit their manor house."

"Did you tell the King any of this?" Meikah asked.

Shade shook his head. "I only told him we were following up on reports that sorcerers captured Mezeth's mate."

Kellan took Meikah's empty plate from her. "Leave a letter with Isha. Let her know where we're going and that she can take it to Cryptic Ramblings. Obscure Texts And Scrolls."

"A bookshop?" Meikah asked.

"The assassins prefer to use bookshops to hide their locations. It's the perfect cover. What better place to go when seeking knowledge?" Kellan turned to Shade. "We'll meet you outside as soon as we're ready."

"I'll arrange horses for us." Shade climbed out the window.

Meikah made her way to the study where she wrote a letter for Isha asking her to deliver it to the bookshop and to let the Assassins Of The Dead know they were searching the director of the Sorcerer Academy's manor house. Putting it in writing made it seem like a terrible idea. Not only was he powerful in skill, but he was also powerful because of the people who'd stand by his side.

After folding the letter she gave it to Isha, who she found in the kitchen talking to the housekeeper. Isha gave a single nod as she slipped the letter into a pocket. "You'll be going sightseeing now?"

Meikah smiled, glancing at the housekeeper before she nodded.

Isha squeezed Meikah's hand. "Be careful out there. A city can be a dangerous place."

"I could tell you stories about some of the bad elements we've had around Port Mayren. The King and his guards and soldiers soon take care of them. Why even the directors of all the academies stand by the King when required," the housekeeper said.

Meikah smiled weakly. That was the last thing she'd wanted to hear. "I'll be back tomorrow. We're staying the night with friends."

"When tomorrow?" Isha asked.

"By midday." At least she hoped they'd be done well before then.

"Send word if you'll be late," Isha said.

"I will." With another smile, this one a better attempt than the last one, Meikah returned to her room to dress in her travel outfit.

Shade stood by her window. "When I collected horses from headquarters, I learned your battle gear was ready." He nodded towards the bed.

Meikah stared at the leather and dark cloth outfit, a navy so dark it was nearly black, not sure if she was happy to finally have it.

"Guess you can quit worrying about dying now. That's not a bad outfit to spend an eternity in if you don't want to go to the trouble of altering your clothes."

Meikah spun to face Kellan who stood behind her. "I don't want to die no matter what I'm wearing."

Kellan grinned. "Good to hear." He glanced at the bed. "We'll let you get dressed and meet you out the side of the house. Leave by the window."

"I'll take the horses around to the side." Shade left through the window.

Meikah grabbed Kellan's hand before he could walk away, tugging him back to her. "Someone needs to tell the King about his son."

"You're the one with a dragon to protect you," Kellan said.

"Absolutely not." She let go of his hand, backing away. "I don't think it works like that."

Kellan kept pace with her. "I think Mezeth would face down armies if they insulted her dragon touched."

She placed a hand on his chest to prevent him from coming closer. "I don't think Mezeth needs any excuse to take on armies. She's not impressed with humans. Not that I can blame her."

Kellan placed his hand over Meikah's keeping it pressed against his chest. "I would face armies for you."

Meeting his gaze, she was lost for words.

Kellan raised her hand to his lips. "No matter your choices. Even if you deny what's between us."

She wanted to protest that there was nothing between them, but it would have been a lie. Thoughts of Rafe entered her mind and she pushed them aside too. "I need to get ready." She tugged her hand from his light grip.

Kellan grinned. "You can run as far and as often as you want. It doesn't change anything." He strode from the room, closing the door behind him.

Meikah stared at the timber door for several minutes before she could bring herself to change into her battle gear. It fit perfectly, the supple leather armour more comfortable than she would have expected. Collecting her weapons and putting on her half-face mask, she headed out the window.

The moment he spotted her, Kellan mounted his horse, taking the reins of the third horse from Shade and leading it over to her. She took the reins from him and swung into the saddle, following the two of them as they headed along the coast. None of them spoke and Meikah found herself regularly checking over her shoulder, half expecting to find Jelena or Neven behind them. No one followed and eventually they came into sight of the director's manor house, remaining hidden amongst a grove of trees.

Meikah stared at it open-mouthed for a moment. "One could almost believe he wishes he lived in a castle."

"Or he has plans to one day move into a castle," Shade suggested.

A shiver ran through Meikah. "Is that possible?"

Kellan nodded. "He's a relative of the King's. A cousin or second cousin. Something like that."

Meikah's grip tightened on the reins. "We're only guessing. We don't know anything for certain."

Shade nodded towards the manor house. "We know something for certain. Either he's highly paranoid and expecting to be attacked or there's something rather valuable he wants to protect with how many guards he has on duty."

Chapter Twenty-Three

Meikah's gaze was drawn to each of the guards she could see. She counted thirty of them before she stopped counting. There had to be easily double that. "How do you know that's not the typical amount of guards that manor houses have in this area?"

Kellan grinned, glancing at Shade. "Oh, he'd know."

"We don't have time for this. We need to find a way inside and see if we can find Galzeren," Shade said.

Meikah wished they did have the time for her to ask what Kellan was referring to, but the sun was getting low on the horizon and would set within a couple of hours. "How do we get in there? It looks impossible."

Kellan's gaze remained on the manor house. "Maybe we don't have to get in there. I wonder if

Mezeth can sense her mate like Letha could sense her egg."

Meikah turned to Kellan. "Do you think that's possible?"

Kellan shrugged. "It might be worth finding out. The director's manor house isn't exactly a small place to search."

"What will it be?" Shade asked. "Breaking in to the manor house or speaking with Mezeth?"

Meikah didn't hesitate. "Speaking with Mezeth." If they could avoid having to get past all the guards, they might manage to locate Galzeren before midday tomorrow. That was if he was at the manor house.

With a single nod, Shade turned his horse towards the city. Again the journey was silent and they'd nearly reached Port Mayren when sixteen hooded figures stepped out of the cover provided by the trees lining the road.

"Did you think we'd let you survive after what you did to our family?" Jelena demanded.

Shade drew his daggers, leaping from his horse. "Don't kill them." He attacked the nearest figure.

Meikah barely had time to dismount and draw her weapons before she was being attacked, surrounded and unable to protest Shade's order. Not that she wanted to kill anyone, but it was hard when those fighting you were determined to end your life.

Jelena joined those attacking Shade. "It won't make any difference. We'll continue to keep coming after you until you're dead."

Lightning flashed along Meikah's blades as she was driven backwards, struggling to avoid the various weapons used against her.

"Move in close," Shade ordered.

Meikah had no idea how she was expected to do that. The hooded figures drove her further away from Kellan and Shade. "I can't."

Kellan fought through the crowd, swinging his sword and blocking with his dagger as he made his way towards her. "Over here, Shade."

A gust of air pushed some of the attackers back and Meikah could reach Kellan's side. Back to back, she fought off the hooded figures as they regained their balance and came in for the kill.

Shade forced his way to them, Jelena close on his heels. As he reached Meikah and Kellan, he sheathed his daggers and raised his hands. A solid wall of air pushed all the hooded figures from them. Shade staggered, going to his knees as he held the wall of air around them, the hooded figures trying to break through.

"You could have done that to start with," Kellan said.

"Needed to see their strength first." As Shade spoke, the wall buckled and bent as the attackers continued to try and reach them.

"Let Neven through." Kellan held his weapons ready.

"No," Jelena yelled. "Three against one isn't fair."

The air eased around Neven and he stumbled into the small, protected area, daggers drawn and warily watching them.

Kellan grinned. "The two of us. You beat me then you can fight Shade next. One on one."

"I'm the oldest," Jelena said. "I should be the one to fight."

"If he fails, you can have a turn next," Kellan offered.

Neven remained where he was.

"The offer won't last. Better make the most of it while you can," Kellan said.

Meikah was studying Shade, worried about how long he'd hold the circle, when Neven attacked. The fight was over in minutes, Neven pinned to the ground, his daggers lying out of reach and Kellan's blade at his throat.

"Do you concede?" Kellan demanded.

"No." Neven glared up at Kellan.

"Would you rather die?" Kellan asked.

Neven remained silent.

The hooded figures had ceased attacking, all watching what happened within the circle of air. Jelena continued to hold her daggers. "You promised me a turn if my brother failed."

"I didn't fail," Neven protested.

Kellan chuckled. "It looks that way to me. Do I need to end your life to show you how badly you failed?"

"Let him live," Shade ordered.

Kellan sheathed his dagger and dragged Neven to his feet, pushing him towards the wall of air. It eased around him and then he was outside, Jelena entering in his place. Kellan drew his dagger as he faced her.

Meikah picked up the two daggers Neven had left behind, not wanting to leave them where they might be used against one of them. She glanced at Shade before returning her attention to the fight, still worried about how long he could hold the wall of air. From the look of him, it wouldn't be much longer.

Kellan met each of Jelena's attacks, making none of his own. The two of them fought fiercely, none of those outside the circle of air looking away. The circle shrank a few inches, but still the two of them fought.

Meikah looked from Shade to the hooded figures he held at bay. The moment the air dissipated, they'd join the fight. She studied Kellan and Jelena. They were too evenly matched when it came to a straight fight. If he didn't do something else soon, Shade wouldn't be able to keep protecting them.

Kellan grinned. "You're a better fighter than your brother."

"I've trained longer than him." Jelena didn't pause in her attacks.

"There's only one problem with your skills." Kellan blocked each of her moves.

"I don't see any problem." Jelena increased the speed of her attacks.

"You have no magic." Kellan dodged her attack, moving past her as the ground around her became muddy.

Jelena struggled to remain on her feet. She would have managed if Kellan hadn't followed up by attacking with his sword. She crashed to the ground, mud splattering everyone, losing hold of one of her daggers as she tried to break her fall.

He stood over her, his foot on her wrist to prevent her from using her other dagger against him and his sword at her throat. "Are you bright enough to concede? Or are you going to claim you haven't lost, like your brother did."

"Why won't you kill me?" Jelena demanded.

"Do you want to die?" Kellan kept his sword at her throat.

Chapter Twenty-Four

Meikah wanted to beg Kellan to hurry. Shade was pale with the strain of holding the circle of air in place.

"I'm not suicidal if that's what you're asking," Jelena said. "I want to know why you'd spare us."

Kellan nodded towards Shade. "I'm not the one who said to let you live."

Jelena stared up at Kellan for a moment before she spoke. "I concede for today. They'll let you go unharmed."

Kellan sheathed his weapons and held a hand out to Jelena, moving his foot off her wrist.

"No," Neven protested.

Jelena took Kellan's hand, allowing him to pull her to her feet. Letting go of his hand, she faced her brother. "Anyone who raises a weapon against these three today, will face me."

Neven's eyes narrowed. "The day ends at midnight."

Jelena inclined her head.

Neven smiled. One filled with the promise of retribution. "I agree."

When there were murmurs of agreement and nods from the rest of the attackers, Shade lowered the circle of air. Kellan helped him to his feet, slinging an arm around his shoulders.

Neven stopped in front of Meikah, standing far too close for her comfort. She held her ground, meeting his angry gaze.

He held out a hand. "My weapons."

With the way he spoke to her, Meikah wanted to tell him there was no way she'd return them. But she didn't want the fighting to resume. Before she could return the daggers, Kellan spoke.

"I'm not sure he really wants them. Either that, or he has no idea how to ask for something."

"Neven." There was a warning note to Jelena's tone.

He continued to glare at Meikah, but his voice, when he spoke, was devoid of emotion. "Could you please return my weapons? They belonged to my father."

Meikah handed them over, not taking her gaze

off him. She didn't trust him in the slightest. Several comments came to mind, but she kept them to herself. She didn't need to make the situation worse.

"Guess you should be more careful where you leave them," Kellan said.

Meikah wanted to groan at the anger that flared in Neven's eyes. She didn't doubt that after midnight he'd be coming after not only Shade, but her and Kellan too.

"Time to go," Jelena ordered.

Meikah remained where she was until the three of them were alone on the road. She turned to face her companions, shocked at how exhausted Shade looked. "We can wait until-"

Shade interrupted her. "There isn't time to wait." He stepped away from Kellan, staggering. "You catch the horses."

Meikah slipped an arm around Shade's waist. "You'll be lucky if you can manage to ride."

Shade smiled briefly. "That I should be able to manage. Anything else, I doubt it." He looked to where Kellan was catching the horses, none of them having gone far. "The two of you will have to continue alone. I'll return to headquarters."

Meikah wanted to protest, but even if he was

willing, there was no way he'd be capable of helping. "Should we ride to the bookshop with you?"

Shade shook his head, stepping away from her when Kellan brought the horses over. He needed help to mount, Kellan giving the reins to Meikah to hold. Slumping in the saddle, Shade looked down at Meikah. "Be careful what you say to the King. He might not be as volatile as some of his ancestors, but he's still the King."

Kellan took the reins of his horse from Meikah, grinning up at Shade. "Don't get caught."

Shade smiled, this one lasting longer than the previous one. "You are the two that need to worry about not getting caught." With a nod to them, he rode towards the city.

Meikah waited until he was out of hearing before she spoke. "How are we going to manage this with just the two of us?"

Kellan swung into the saddle. "I guess we're about to find out."

When they reached the location where they were taken to the previous night, to meet with Mezeth, the guards refused to allow them to enter. Even showing their Assassins Of The Dead medallions didn't help.

"We are here on business of the King's," Kellan

stated. "Fetch someone who can let us in. He told us his people would give us what help we needed."

The two guards shared a look before one of them spoke. "No one said anything to me when I came on duty today."

"The King should have given us something to prove we can enter." Kellan grinned at Meikah. "Especially since the two of you are on first name terms."

Meikah wanted to protest the speculative look that came into the guards' eyes at Kellan's words. She made do with glaring at Kellan.

He grinned back at her before turning to the guards. "Do you really want to lose your jobs over this? What can it hurt to send for someone who'll let you know that we're meant to be here?"

Again the guards shared a look, but this time it contained doubt. Eventually one of them nodded and entered the door they guarded, returning a few minutes later to let them in.

A guard waited for them on the other side of the door and led them to the cell Mezeth was being kept in. It was a different one to before. At their approach, she uncurled from the bed of gold and jewels she slept on.

"Did you find him?"

Meikah glanced at the guard, not sure what she should say while he was nearby.

"You may go," Mezeth ordered the guard.

He bowed before retreating.

Mezeth turned to Meikah once he was out of sight. "Did you find my mate?"

"We have news of him." Meikah passed along Daveth's message, placing her hand against Mezeth's forehead when the dragon lowered her head. "I'm sorry. But at least it means he was alive when he was taken from the island."

Mezeth raised her head, dislodging Meikah's hand. "It doesn't mean he still lives though. And what of Daveth. You said he's a spirit. Did he tell you what happened to him and his companions?"

Kellan was the one to briefly explain what had happened.

"There was an assassination attempt on Timell that year." The King stood in the doorway, entering the cell when they all looked towards him. "Necromancers raised armies of the dead, training them to fight in preparation of facing my grandfather's army. The leaders were captured and imprisoned for an eternity. Many of those who followed them escaped to the Arcton Mountains from where they came. They were sick of being driven from towns and decided they'd take back what they'd lost."

"Why have we never heard about it?" Kellan asked.

"Everyone thought at the time it was best to remove all records of it in case necromancers thought it a good idea to try again in the future," the King said.

"But they lost," Meikah said. "Wouldn't it have been better to leave the information in the history books so they knew it wasn't possible?"

"There's the problem. They came very close to winning. Leaving any record of it would allow them to see where they could have improved their revolt." The King paused a moment. "Not that I blame them for fighting to take back what they'd lost due to circumstances beyond their control." He looked from Meikah to Kellan. "Do you have news of Mezeth's mate?"

Meikah wished now that they'd asked Mezeth about what she was capable of first. "We don't know exactly where he is. What we were hoping was that Mezeth might sense him if she was close enough. Like a dragon can sense their egg."

"I would have to be extremely close," Mezeth said. "Not all dragons would be capable, but we've been together enough years I should be able to sense him if I'm within fifty feet of him."

Meikah tried to contain her disappointment. Some parts of the manor house were taller than that. What if he was in a basement or dungeon beneath one of the taller sections? Would that make it impossible for Mezeth to sense him?

"I can't allow it," the King said.

Mezeth lowered her head to meet the King's gaze. "You would stop me from going after my mate?"

"I can't allow you to attack my people in search of your mate," the King stated.

Smoke curled from Mezeth's nostrils. "You think you could stop me from leaving? I could kill you before any of your guards reach me."

The King held his ground. "These two are mine. They would stop you."

"You're wrong. One of them is mine." Mezeth growled, more smoke rising from her nostrils.

"All the Assassins Of The Dead answer first to me," the King said.

"No dragon touched answers to a mere king."

Meikah wanted to beg the two of them to stop. She didn't want to be caught up in their argument. But she had no idea what she could say that wouldn't have them turning their anger on her instead of each other.

"Then she'll need to choose," the King said. "I expect the loyalty of all my subjects."

Chapter Twenty-Five

Panic raced through Meikah. She didn't want to be chased not only from her home, but also her country. She blurted out the first words that came to mind. "Your son may be involved."

The King spun to face her. "I beg your pardon?"

Meikah took a step back from him. "Not deliberately. Or at least not as far as we can tell."

"You'd best tell me everything you know," the King ordered.

"We don't know anything for certain," Kellan said. "That's why we're hoping Mezeth can go with us."

"You think I should let the dragon freely roam my country after the amount of devastation she's caused," the King said.

"I think even a human would have done similar in their grief," Kellan said.

"They might have," the King said. "But a dragon is capable of more devastation than a single human."

"Maybe the humans you know." Kellan grinned fleetingly. "I've seen the destruction a single human can do and it can rival that of a grieving dragon."

"I'm not talking about necromancers." The King made a sweeping gesture towards the exit. "I'm talking about the ordinary citizen."

Kellan met the King's gaze. "It only takes a single person to create a mob."

The King didn't answer immediately, eventually inclining his head. "What do you suggest? And who is it you think is guilty?"

Meikah feared how he'd react if she answered him with the truth. "Someone with not only a great deal of power, but high standing."

"Which is why we don't want to mention names, in case things aren't the way they appear," Kellan said.

"You expect me to trust you." The King nodded towards Meikah. "Even after I've been informed that one who I should be able to trust above all others, isn't mine to command."

Kellan took a step towards the King. "Our faction has never been yours to command. We work for the good of all. We play no favourites, not even for royalty."

Meikah wanted to drag Kellan back when she saw the flare of anger in the King's eyes.

"A name. Give me a name and I'll allow the dragon to leave here under your care."

"I am not some hatchling that needs watching over." Smoke continued to curl from Mezeth's nostrils.

Kellan met the King's gaze. "I believe he's saying we'll be held responsible for anything you do wrong and be punished accordingly."

The King inclined his head.

"No one is to punish the dragon touched other than a dragon of high standing," Mezeth stated.

After one more look at Kellan, the King faced Mezeth. "Anyone remaining a citizen of my country is subject to the laws of this land."

Worried she was about to be banished from the country, Meikah stepped between Mezeth and the King. "Please. Enough. You both asked for my help. All I want to do is find Galzeren. And the person responsible for capturing him. Not to accuse anyone who might be innocent."

"Then name the person who might be innocent and give me your promise Mezeth will kill no one while seeking her mate. The captain of my guards is also to go with you as a witness to who is innocent and who is guilty."

Meikah wanted to groan at the King's words. How many more demands would he have if they took too long to settle the issue? "The captain can come with us and I'll take responsibility for Mezeth's actions until she begins her journey home."

"Not good enough," the King said. "I will have that name."

"The director of the Sorcerer Academy," Kellan said.

Meikah held her breath at the silence that filled the cell, the King staring at Kellan. She wanted to demand what he was thinking, but had more than overstepped her bounds as it was. She expelled her breath in a rush of air when the King inclined his head. "You're happy with those terms?"

The King studied her for a moment. "I'm far from happy. You accuse one of my most loyal subjects of a crime that can be punished by death depending on the severity of it."

"I'm sorry." Meikah continued to hold his gaze.

"You might be sorry, but I've noticed neither of you have retracted the accusation."

Meikah didn't reply, only continued to meet his gaze.

"We can leave now?" Mezeth asked.

The King faced Mezeth. "In my country, murder is punishable by death."

The smoke rising from Mezeth's nostrils thickened. "So too in my world. You had best hope Galzeren lives."

"Your dragon touched had best hope that too." The King strode towards the doorway, pausing before he left the cell. "I'll send a guard for the captain and have him meet you outside."

"Tell him to bring a mask with him," Kellan called after the King.

Meikah stared at the empty doorway, trying not to think of everything that could go wrong. The worst being that she could be blamed for murder if Mezeth killed someone. Why had she agreed to be held responsible for the dragon's actions? That had been completely crazy. The words that the woman at the ball had spoken came to mind. Maybe she'd been right and she was foolish.

"Do you plan to stand here the rest of the night?" Mezeth demanded. "Galzeren is still in danger."

Taking a deep breath, and slowly letting it out, Meikah faced Mezeth. "I'm ready to leave when you are."

Mezeth lifted her head, looking down her nose at Meikah. "Lead the way."

Taking another deep breath, Meikah stepped out of the cell. She soon found it was impossible to take Mezeth out the way they'd come in and a guard had to show them another way out. By the time they stepped outside, the captain was waiting for them, mounted on a horse.

He waited until the three of them were riding away from the city, Mezeth flying well overhead, before he spoke. "The King said you accused the director of the Sorcerer Academy of breaking the law."

"We accused no one," Kellan said. "We pointed out that he might be innocent. Our findings point towards him, but that doesn't mean he's guilty of anything other than being in the wrong place at the wrong time."

"He'd never do anything like that," the captain said.

"Do you know him personally?" Meikah asked.

"He's my wife's uncle. I've sat across the table from him many a time."

Meikah drew in a sharp breath at the captain's words. Could things get any worse? She dreaded to think how the captain would react if the director was guilty.

The rest of the journey was made in silence and

they stopped in the same grove of trees they'd stopped in last time, all of them dismounting. Mezeth flew down to land in front of them, just outside the tree line.

"This is the place you would have me search?"

Meikah looked from Mezeth to the fortified manor house. It no longer seemed like such a good idea. "They'll see you."

"That doesn't mean they'll be able to catch me." Mezeth spread her wings, leaping into the air.

Chapter Twenty-Six

Meikah ran out of the cover of the trees. "Don't kill anyone." She stared after the dragon who hadn't answered her.

Kellan tugged her back into cover. "They may patrol the area."

"There's no need for them to patrol the area," the captain said. "We keep the roads around here safe."

Kellan gestured towards the manor house. "In that case, why are there so many guards and soldiers making the place look like it's ready for war."

The captain slowly shook his head. "There must be a logical explanation for it."

Kellan faced the captain, turning his back on the manor house. "Yeah. They're keeping a dragon somewhere over there."

Shouts rang out from the manor house and fire and lightning lit up the area as sorcerers attacked

Mezeth. Meikah clasped her hands together as the dragon dodged the attacks, flying in low to the ground and close to the buildings. Relief rushed through her when Mezeth didn't attack, flying towards the ocean before circling around and heading back towards the grove of trees.

Mezeth landed in front of them. "It's impossible for me to search the entire place."

Meikah stepped forward, resting a hand against the dragon's scales. "Are you unharmed?"

Mezeth lowered her head, touching her forehead to Meikah's. She didn't speak until she raised her head again. "You seem to be lacking in training, but your heart is in the right place. I'm unharmed. That isn't what's important. What is important is finding out if Galzeren is imprisoned in that place. You'll need to search for me."

"The place is a fortress," Meikah protested.

"I'll take out any who harm you," Mezeth said.

"That would be murder," the captain warned.

"What if Mezeth distracts them while we sneak in?" Kellan suggested.

The captain stared at him. "You want to break into the home of the director of the Sorcerer Academy."

Kellan gave a half shrug. "Seems preferable to

killing everyone down there just in case they're guilty."

"Decide quickly," Mezeth said. "My mate has been missing for too long."

Meikah took a deep breath, straightening her shoulders. She didn't want to be held responsible for murder. Nor did she want anyone who was innocent to be killed. "I'll sneak in there."

"I will distract them for you." Mezeth took to the sky.

Kellan moved to Meikah's side. "We'll sneak in there."

"I'm not about to let you go down there on your own," the captain protested.

"Did you bring a mask with you?" Kellan tied the reins of his horse to a tree. "We don't want them knowing who you are if we're spotted."

After tying the reins of his horse to a tree, the captain took out a full-face mask. "The King informed me."

"Have you visited the director's manor house before?" Kellan asked.

"You expect me to give you a tour of the place?" the captain asked incredulously.

Kellan grinned. "I doubt we'll have time for that. I

was thinking more along the lines of you showing us the places big enough to keep a dragon."

"The old dungeons. They're storage rooms now," the captain said.

Kellan waved the captain ahead of him. "Lead the way."

The captain pulled on his mask before striding towards the manor house. As he drew closer, his steps slowed. Several times Kellan had to draw him into hiding places when he would have walked through areas where he risked being discovered.

Kellan drew the captain back against the wall surrounding the manor house. "They didn't all chase after Mezeth." He nodded towards a guard at the front entrance. "We'll need to go over the wall."

The captain looked upwards. "Boost me up then."

Kellan cupped his hands and helped the captain onto the top of the wall, turning to Meikah next. "Ready?"

She doubted telling him 'no' would make a difference. Stepping onto his cupped hands, she reached for the top of the wall, surprised when the captain grabbed hold of her hand and drew her up with him. He reached down to help Kellan up before he took hold of her hand again and lowered her to the ground on the other side.

Seeing a guard coming towards them, Meikah sent lightning into the weapon he rested a hand against as well as into the ground behind him where it made a low cracking sound. She smiled when the guard spun to look behind him, having let go of the hilt of his sword. While he was distracted, she raced towards the manor house, pressing herself against the wall. She looked between the guard and her companions, ready to use her lightning if he turned before they reached her side.

Kellan reached her first, the captain seconds behind him and stepping around the two of them to make his way along the building. He stopped at a window partway along the side. "None are to be harmed."

"We'll leave them alive, but we can't promise they won't be harmed if they attack us." Kellan reached for the window.

The captain grabbed his hand, preventing him from opening it. "You will harm no one. They're perfectly within their rights to protect this property."

"Then what do you suggest we do?" Kellan asked. "Lie down and die for them?" He grinned, turning to Meikah. "Good thing you're wearing your battle outfit."

She didn't bother telling Kellan she didn't want to die regardless of what she wore. "We don't want to hurt them. But we're not about to let them kill us and there's no other way to discover if the director captured the dragon."

Kellan pulled his hand out of the captain's grip. "If you don't want the guard coming this way to be harmed, then you better let us get out of sight."

The captain glanced past Meikah before opening the window. "We shouldn't be here. The director wouldn't go against the King in this matter. He has too much to lose."

Kellan waited until they were all inside the lavishly furnished drawing room before he spoke. "Show us where the dungeon is so we can find out for certain if he's guilty or innocent."

"The King should have asked him to show him around, not used these underhanded methods." The captain strode from the room.

Meikah hurried after him, tempted to tell him not to get caught. With how he strode through the hallways, it was like he dared someone to find them.

The captain started to step into another hallway, having led them through several. Drawing back, he stumbled into Meikah. "There are four guards at the entrance to the dungeon."

"Is that typical?" Kellan asked.

The captain didn't answer immediately. "No."

"How are we to get past them?" Meikah asked.

Kellan drew his weapons, grinning. "Only one way I know of."

The captain placed his hand on Kellan's arm. "Don't kill anyone." When Kellan nodded, he took out a vial. "The potion allowing me to see in the dark will wear off shortly. Just because most of these hallways are lit up, doesn't mean the dungeon will be too."

They waited until he'd drunk the potion before stepping out into the next hallway, all of them with weapons drawn. The guards instantly drew their weapons, running towards them, slipping over in puddles that formed on the floor.

"Go ahead." Kellan glanced at Meikah. "We'll take care of this lot."

Meikah ran past him, flinging the door open. She stumbled backwards when she saw another four guards. "Who will take care of these ones?" She blocked a sword, throwing herself to the side when one of them threw a fireball at her.

Kellan joined her, mist swirling around him and spreading out through the hallway and dungeon entrance. "How about we try that earlier trick?" The mist surrounded the guards, leaving a large space around them. Moisture formed on everything it touched.

"What if it kills them?" The lightning automatically flared along her blades as she blocked another attack.

"You planning to lie down and die for them?" Kellan fought three of the guards, slowly retreating to where the captain tried to hold off the other four.

Chapter Twenty-Seven

"Retreat." Meikah drew on her magic, waiting until her and Kellan weren't in contact with the four guards before flinging lightning at them. Light flashed and a loud crack sounded, ringing out in the hallway. The guards were flung backwards.

The guards fighting the captain bolted. He strode towards them. "I told you not to kill anyone."

Kellan knelt beside a guard. "This one lives. She knocked him out." He rose to his feet. "We need to see what they're guarding before they bring back reinforcements."

The captain checked the other three before he followed them into the dungeons.

Meikah couldn't resist asking the question she wasn't sure she wanted answered. "Are they alive?"

"Yes." The captain's tone was sharp and abrupt.

Meikah didn't blame him. She hadn't wanted to

hurt any of them. Like he'd pointed out, they'd been guarding the place from intruders. "Thank you."

"For what?" The captain glanced over his shoulder at her.

"Checking." She hadn't been able to bring herself to find out.

He glanced over his shoulder at her again, this time saying nothing.

Kellan, who was in the lead, reached an intersection. "Where to now?"

"Take a left. It leads to a large area that also has access from outside. The only way it'd be possible to get a dragon down here."

Kellan went left, striding along the empty corridor, his footsteps almost silent. "How long do you think we'll have before the guards can bring reinforcements?"

"Five minutes more at the most." The captain tried to open the door at the end of the corridor. "It's locked."

"Let me have a go." Kellan sheathed his sword and placed his hand over the lock. A minute later, the door swung open. He didn't have time to draw his sword before he was under attack by four guards.

"Don't use the same attack as–" the captain broke off as he fought his way into the room.

Meikah entered, about to join the fight when she saw what had caused the captain to break off mid-sentence. She stared, stunned by the sight of a dragon who was chained and lying in the middle of the spacious room. Relief rushed through her when she saw he still breathed, his sides rising and falling. A sleep spell had been cast over the front half of him and scales had been torn from his body leaving bloody patches behind. There were rusty marks on the floor around him along with fresh splatters of blood. He was in bad shape, but alive.

Kellan shoved Meikah out of the way of an oncoming sword. "Help him. We've got this lot."

Meikah shook her head, trying not to think of how much pain the dragon must be in. Before she could take another step, the sound of running footsteps along the hallway drew her attention. Guards came towards them. She ran to the door, slamming it shut. "I can't lock it. There must be over a dozen guards out there."

"Fuse the lock with lightning." Kellan fought two of the guards, mist forming around him again.

"Use the earlier attack," the captain ordered.

Meikah backed away from the door, striking the lock with her lightning several times. The doorknob turned, she again struck it with lightning. A yelp sounded on the other side of the door and the knob sprang back to normal position. When the doorknob rattled again, she struck it once more, backing away from it. Again the guard on the other side let go with a yelp.

"Forget about the door. Give us a hand." The captain was pinned against a wall, the two guards able to use magic.

Meikah raced across the room to help with the guards, trying not to think about what would happen if the guards on the other side of the door managed to get it open. She attacked one of the guards, striking him with lightning when mist surrounded him. Spinning to face Kellan, she did the same to another one of the guards when she was encircled with mist.

"We can manage these two. See what you can do about the dragon," Kellan said.

Meikah crossed the room to stand beside the dragon. She had no idea what was keeping the sleep spell in place, but it gave her an idea. "Force the guards over here." She gestured towards the spell.

Grinning, Kellan tried to do what Meikah had suggested, the guard trying to avoid being caught in the spell. When he failed yet again, he tackled the guard sending him flying into the spell, partially caught in it himself.

Meikah dragged him out of the spell, fighting against the tiredness that washed over her. She barely had time to step out of the way of the other guard that the captain drove into the spell with his non-stop attacks. The door shuddered and she faced it. "How are we meant to get the dragon out of here before they break down the door? It sounds like a battering ram or something."

"I'll get the exit door opened," Kellan said.

"They might be out there too," the captain warned.

"There's no way I can drag a dragon across the ground." Meikah stared at the large, bloody creature. What they needed was Rafe. He was the only one capable of moving a dragon. Her mouth slowly opened. "Mezeth. We need Mezeth." She ran to Kellan's side in time to see him open the door slightly.

"Out of the way." Kellan had barely given a warning when the door burst open, guards and sorcerers pouring inside.

"Who do you think you are?" A sorcerer stepped through the crowd.

"That's the director." The captain stood beside Meikah, his words soft.

Kellan stepped in front of Meikah. "Get outside and call Mezeth." Mist formed around them, quickly thickening. "Lucky we're so close to the ocean with all its moisture to draw from."

"Think you can use that trick against me?" The director sent a gust of wind towards Kellan.

The mist separated, much of it holding and thickening around Meikah and the area surrounding her. She inched to the side, not sure how she'd get past all those between her and the door. A smile slowly formed. She didn't need to get past them. Raising her hand, she focused on her magic, trying to call on the lacey dragon. Lightning streaked out from her hand, but nothing else. Her smile faded when sorcerers blocked the lightning from escaping the room.

The director laughed. "Is that all the two of you are capable of? What about your companion? Or is he some useless warrior?"

The captain didn't answer, only readied his sword, his stance wide.

Fear raced through Meikah. This was worse than anything they'd ever faced. The two of them couldn't manage alone. Or three if she counted the captain who was severely lacking in the skills needed to face a sorcerer.

"We need Mezeth," Kellan said.

Meikah wanted to demand how she was meant to

do that. They were outnumbered, the door behind them continued to shudder and she had no idea how to call the lacey dragon let alone the living one. Maybe she should have taken Daveth up on his offer to train her. As bad an idea as that had seemed at the time, it now looked a lot better than this.

"Give up and throw down your weapons and I'll make sure it's a painless death," the director offered.

Meikah tightened her grip on her weapons. Giving up wouldn't help. Necromancers couldn't die even if they lost their body.

"I won't make this offer again," the director warned.

"Good," Kellan said. "We weren't interested in hearing it the first time." Mist figures rose around them, filling the area with what looked like armed warriors.

One of them merged with Meikah and when they advanced, she did too, a small glimmer of hope forming. Before it became too great, the director raised a strong wind that cut through the mist, causing the warriors to vanish one at a time. The ones in front of her shredded into nothing. Having nothing to lose, she ran forward, raising her sword, lightning leaping from the blade to strike the nearest sorcerer. When a fireball flew towards her, Meikah blocked it with her sword, the heat of it causing her to drop the weapon. Fingers splayed, hand held out, when another fireball came at her, the lacey dragon burst forth, colliding with the flames and scattering them. It cut straight through the crowd and into the sky.

"Call her." Kellan blocked fireballs and dodged lightning.

Chapter Twenty-Eight

Meikah continued to run forward, pushing her way through the sorcerers, another lacey dragon helping clear the way. "Mezeth!" The lacey dragon raced into the sky.

A roar filled the night, flames bursting from the dragon who flew low, scattering those who'd followed Meikah. "My mate. Where's my mate?"

Meikah tried to dodge an attack, stumbling to land sprawled on the ground. "Inside." She rolled onto her back, clutching her dagger as a guard loomed over her, sword raised.

Mezeth landed beside Meikah, swatting the guard to the ground. "What have they done to him? Why can't I sense him?"

Scrambling to her feet, Meikah faced the sorcerers and guards who'd turned towards the dragon. "He's mostly in a sleep spell."

"Set him free while I see that these ones pay for their crimes." Mezeth stalked towards the sorcerers and guards.

"He's too heavy for me to move and you promised you wouldn't kill anyone." Meikah walked at the dragon's side, the silhouette of the dragon clearly visible on the back of her hand.

A rumbling growl rose up from Mezeth's chest. "I'm about to start my journey home. Do you all hear that? Now I have my mate, I can begin my journey home."

The director slowly backed away, his guards and sorcerers now in front of him. "Kill the dragon. We'll have the live one for blood and scales and the dead one for flesh and bones."

They all attacked at once, the director retreating as they did. Meikah ran after him, leaving Mezeth to fight the rest. She scooped up her sword as she ran past it, catching up to the director as he reached the imprisoned dragon.

Kellan joined her, his sword pointed at the director. "Release him from the sleep spell and we'll offer you a painless death."

Meikah grinned at his words. "We won't offer it again."

"You can't kill him," the captain protested.

The director stared at the captain. "You would betray me like this? I've treated you like family."

"I had believed you innocent," the captain said. "You're the one who betrayed all of us."

"The King is the one who's betrayed his people. He keeps us weak by punishing us if we use dragon parts in our spells and potions. Look at how powerful they are." The director made a vague motion towards his people who fought Mezeth, many of them remaining motionless on the ground. "We're insignificant compared to them. Let me pass so I can get some of the powerful spells I've created. Then we'll see who wins. And I can assure you it won't be the dragon."

"He's not going to end the sleep spell," Kellan said.

"Never." The director tried to get past them.

Meikah dashed forward, attacking with her sword and preventing his escape. "We can't let you kill the dragons."

"They'll kill all of us. It's only a matter of time." The director launched a fireball, quickly following it with lightning and a gust of wind that almost knocked Meikah off her feet. "You would cause the death of every last one of us. You and Branok. He's not the king his father was. And no where near the king his great-grandfather was."

"You would have the unrest of earlier reigns?" The

captain attacked the director, blocking the fireball sent at him.

"I would have the power of earlier eras." The director backed away from their attacks, throwing up barriers of air to shield him from their blows.

Remembering how the lacey dragon had formed only when her hand was empty, Meikah sheathed her sword, holding her hand aloft, palm facing the director. It wasn't until he attacked her that the lacey dragon burst forth, lightning crackling across it as it arrowed into the director.

He stumbled back when the lacey dragon breached his defences, slipping on a puddle that formed on the stone floor. He crashed to the ground, caught in the edge of the sleep spell. Struggling to rise, he mumbled some words. Collapsing back onto the ground, he attempted to rise again, once more trying to speak.

The spell vanished and the dragon shook himself as he lumbered to his feet, towering over the director, his chains clanking. "I saw, heard and felt everything. You deserve to have your skin carved from you one piece at a time."

The director tried to back away from the dragon, remaining on the floor. The two guards who'd been caught in the sleep spell also scrambled out of the way.

"He belongs to the King." The captain strode forward to stand in front of Galzeren.

"Mine." Galzeren snatched up the director and flew from the dungeon.

Meikah ran after him, not sure how the King would react to the dragon taking the director. He'd agreed to Mezeth doing what she wished with the culprits if they'd killed her mate, but nothing had been said about Galzeren retaliating. "Galzeren. Please," she called out after him. "Let the King deal with him."

Mezeth roared, flinging guards from her to scoop up Meikah and fly after Galzeren. She came alongside him. "The dragon touched found you for me."

Meikah tried not to look at the ground well below her as she hung from the dragon's claws, the grip surprisingly gentle. "Can we land?"

Galzeren headed for a nearby field, dropping the director in front of him as he landed. "He must feel every bit of pain he caused me."

Meikah rose from the ground where Mezeth had placed her, glancing towards the director. She assumed from what Galzeren had said that the director was unconscious and not dead. "I don't want to be chased from my country. Please let King

Branok have the director. He won't be allowed to escape punishment."

"Do not call him king," Mezeth stated.

Meikah placed her hand against Mezeth's scales. "Please let Branok have him. Let him prove what he'll do to those who break his laws regarding dragons even when they come from powerful families and believe they'll escape with little more than a token punishment."

Mezeth lowered her head to look directly into Meikah's eyes. "You have a good point." She turned to Galzeren. "Let Branok prove his words that none are to harm dragons in his country." A rumbling growl rose from her. "We can go after the sorcerer if Branok fails to keep his promise."

Galzeren glared down at the director. "He deserves to pay." He placed a paw against the director, claws out. "With his flesh stripped from him inch by inch." The tips of his claws pierced the skin.

Meikah took a cautious step towards Galzeren. "He doesn't deserve anyone's mercy for what he's done and I'll make sure the-" She broke off, starting again. "I'll make sure Branok knows of his crimes. Just give him the chance to prove he's a friend of dragons."

Galzeren held Meikah's gaze for a long, drawn out

moment, eventually growling before he lifted his paw from the director. "You will tell him everything."

"Your human who travels with you can easily tell Branok," Mezeth said. "You should come with us."

Chapter Twenty-Nine

Meikah was extremely tempted by Mezeth's offer. There was so much she didn't know about being dragon touched and she had no idea what would happen when she faced the King. "I'm needed elsewhere for now."

"Where will we find you if we have need of you again?" Mezeth asked.

"Dreyton. My home." She started to tell them where to find her parents' home. A smile slowly formed as she realised that Fable was the place she'd thought of when she'd spoken the word 'home'. "You can leave a message for me at Fable. Tomes Of The Arcane. They'll know where I am." They also knew who she was. No wonder she'd instantly thought of Fable. It was the place where she could be herself. Necromancer, dragon touched and templar. "It's my home."

Mezeth inclined her head. "You'll always have a place in our home should you choose. We live further up the Arcton Mountains from the place you humans call King's Peak. We know it as the birthplace of our first ancestor. King Of Dragons."

Galzeren also inclined his head. "You have done me a great service. I am in your debt, dragon touched."

Meikah stepped forward to place her hand against his scales. "There is no debt. It was my privilege to free you." She met his gaze. "Most humans aren't like the director."

"You are young," Galzeren said. "When you've lived the years we have, you'll learn that more are like him than are not."

"If you speak to Marta and Daveth again, tell them we wish they still lived. Their talents and company have been sorely missed," Mezeth said.

"You've learned for certain that they died?" Galzeren asked.

"The dragon touched is also a necromancer," Mezeth said.

Galzeren lowered his head to study Meikah. "How unusual. They're usually warriors."

"I was a templar first," Meikah said.

"Ahh. That makes sense." Galzeren spread his wings. "I wish to put this place behind me."

"How am I meant to get the director to the castle?" Meikah glanced at the motionless figure.

"We'll take you there." Mezeth scooped Meikah up again and flew towards the castle, Galzeren at her side with the director clutched in his claws. They landed on the battlements, startling guards.

Meikah rose to her feet. "Thank you."

Mezeth spread her wings. "Tell Branok I killed none of them. Harmed them, yes. But killed them, no. He isn't to take your life for this evening's doings. If any die from their wounds, they occurred after we began our journey home. But even if any had died while I fought them, I had already claimed my intentions to return home."

Mezeth sprung into the sky before Meikah could reply, Galzeren following his mate after dumping the director on the battlements. Meikah spun to face the guards who held weapons, drawing out the medallion that hung from a leather cord around her neck. She let it fall against her chest. "I need to see the King. Urgently."

Things moved swiftly and Meikah spent hours answering the King's questions, relieved when Kellan and the captain returned to the city and arrived at the castle with their prisoners, bringing the horse she'd ridden with them. When Meikah and Kellan could finally leave, it was midmorning and they made their way to Garven's house, riding the horses Shade had borrowed.

Meikah was relieved to find Shade waiting for them, having been about to set out to learn what had happened to them when he'd heard they weren't back yet. He said he'd return the horses, after they briefly told him about everything, and that he'd lie low until it was time to return to Dreyton.

Heading inside, Meikah assured Isha she was safe, taking the letter back from her. She started to head up to her room.

"Meikie?"

She turned to face Isha.

"You're unharmed?"

Meikah nodded. "Only tired."

"Can you tell me anything of what happened?"

Meikah started to shake her head, smiling instead. "Lives were saved."

Isha came forward to crush Meikah to her. "I'm sure they were." Drawing back from Meikah, Isha smiled. "I'll see that a warm bath is prepared for you and make something for you to eat." She looked past

Meikah to where Kellan stood in the doorway. "Food for both of you."

"Thank you." Meikah headed upstairs, Kellan at her side. "What now?"

"We visit the school for wayward students and wait for a reply to the Duke's letter so we can return home." He stopped in front of her door to face her. "And we return to Durnning Island to tell Daveth and Marta what we learned."

Meikah wanted to protest. She dreaded the thought of passing between the rocks again. "They deserve to know. I also have a message for them from Mezeth." Daveth's offer came to mind. It would be impossible to accept. She couldn't imagine what sort of problems it would cause other than they were likely to be drastic. But how else was she to learn about being dragon touched?

Kellan rested his hands on her hips, stepping close. "What are you thinking about?"

Meikah slowly shook her head. "It doesn't matter." She should probably focus on learning about being a necromancer. It would be less dangerous for those around her if she continued to work on those skills. Accepting Daveth's help would be a terrible idea.

Kellan grinned. "You were thinking about me, weren't you?"

Laughter bubbled up, escaping. "Actually, I was thinking about another male." She met his gaze, seeing the humour in his eyes at her words.

He lowered his head. "Are you sure?"

Her laughter faded at the look in his eyes, power instantly filling her, the lightning in her eyes reflected back at her from his. "Honestly?" She paused a moment. "I have no idea."

"That's all right. I can wait until you do." With another grin, he drew away from her, meeting her gaze a moment longer before he strode to his room.

She stared at his door when he closed it behind himself. There might be a lot of things she needed to figure out, but not as many as there once were. When they returned to Dreyton, there would be changes. And not everyone would be happy about them. For now though, they could relax, once they'd visited the island. Galzeren had been found and the director would be punished, along with his daughter and all those who'd knowingly been involved. And the spells and potions he'd created from Galzeren would be destroyed. Their task here was done. Entering her room, Meikah smiled, wondering what task Danton would have for them next. Surely nothing could be as dangerous as this one had been.

Free Ebook

Subscribe to Avril's newsletter and receive a free ebook. This ebook is exclusive to those on her mailing list. To find out more about this offer visit:

www.avrilsabine.com/free-ebook

*

We value your privacy and will not sell, rent, exchange or loan your email address to third parties. Your information is confidential and you are under no obligation to remain on the mailing list and can unsubscribe at any time.

Acknowledgements

Thank you to my usual crew. I couldn't manage without your help.

To The Reader

If you enjoyed this book, why not consider leaving a review to help other readers discover it too? Reader engagement is one of the few ways that lets an author know readers want more books in a particular series or genre. So leave a review and tell friends, not only about this book but also about other ones you've enjoyed, so you can continue to enjoy books by your favourite authors for years to come.

Dreams are meant to be lived,

Avril.

About The Author

Avril is an Australian author who lives with her family on acreage in South East Queensland. She writes mostly young adult and children's speculative fiction, but has been known to dabble in other genres. You can find more information about her at www.avrilsabine.com where you can also subscribe to her newsletter to be kept informed about new releases, current projects, blog posts and exclusive news.

Titles By Avril Sabine

Stories about strong characters and characters who discover their strengths.

SERIES

Assassins Of The Dead- Young Adult Fantasy/ Paranormal

Book 1: Dark Blade

Book 2: Dragon Touched

Book 3: Society Against Vampires

Book 4: King's Request

Dragon Blood- Young Adult Urban Fantasy (with elements of romance)

(5 book series)

Book 1: Pliethin

Book 2: Wyvern

Book 3: Surety

Book 4: Knight

Book 5: Mage

Dragon Mage- Young Adult Urban Fantasy (with elements of romance)

(Series two of Dragon Blood series)

Book 1: Promise

Dragon Blood Chronicles- Young Adult Urban Fantasy (with elements of romance)

(Companion stand alone series to Dragon Blood)

Book 1: Oath

Book 2: Betrayed

Guardians Of The Round Table- Young Adult Fantasy LitRPG

(Co-written with Storm and Rhys Petersen)

Book 1: Dexterity Fail

Book 2: Goblin Boots

Book 3: Singed Feathers

Book 4: Frog Mage

Book 5: Crystal Mine

Book 6: Cursed Harp

Rosie's Rangers- Young Adult Western Steampunk

(6 book series)

Book 1: Justice

Book 2: Vengeance

Book 3: Treachery

Book 4: Accused

Book 5: Wanted

Book 6: Corruption

Mark Of Kings- Children's Fantasy

(Upper middle grade/preteen)

(4 book series)

Book 1: The Arena

Book 2: The Island

Book 3: The Assassin

Book 4: The King

STAND ALONE SERIES

Demon Hunters- Young Adult Urban Fantasy/ Horror (with elements of romance)

Book 1: Blood Sacrifice

Book 2: Retribution

Book 3: Tainted

Book 4: Premonition

Book 5: Cursed

Book 6: Feud

Book 7: Extrication

Plea Of The Damned- *Young Adult Urban Fantasy/Paranormal*

(6 book series)

Book 1: Forgive Me Lucy

Book 2: Forgive Me Aiden

Book 3: Forgive Me Jena

Book 4: Forgive Me Kobe

Book 5: Forgive Me Marti

Book 6: Forgive Me Dawson

Realms Of The Fae- *Young Adult Urban Fantasy* (with elements of romance)

The Sword (short story in Like A Girl Anthology)

Heart Of Stone

Book 1: A Debt Owed

Book 2: Marked By The Hunt

Book 3: The Magic Collector

Book 4: An Unexpected Betrayal

Book 5: Imprisoned By Iron

Fairytales Retold (Short Stories)

Snow-White And Rose-Red

The Twelve Brothers

The Light Princess

Beauty And The Beast

Sleeping Beauty

Aschenputtel

The Golden Bird

The Frog Prince

The Death Of Koshchei The Deathless

Myths And Legends Retold (Short Stories)

Ion, Son Of Apollo

Sir Gawain And The Maid With The Narrow Sleeves

Princess Ilse, The Giant's Daughter

YOUNG ADULT NOVELS

Young Adult Fantasy (with elements of romance)

Elf Sight

Earth Bound

Young Adult Urban Fantasy

Stone Warrior (with elements of romance)

The Jungle Inside

Young Adult Contemporary (with elements of romance)

Through Your Eyes

The Ugly Stepsister

Perfect Little Princess

Young Adult Contemporary/Paranormal

Whispers In The Dark (with elements of romance and same sex relationships)

Over Too Soon (with elements of romance)

Young Adult Sci-Fi

Experiment X-One-Six (Urban Sci-Fi/Superheroes)

An Endless Dawn (Post Apocalyptic Sci-Fi)

CHILDREN'S BOOKS

Dragon Lord (Preteen/early teens) (Fantasy)

The Irish Wizard (Upper middle grade) (Urban Fantasy)

SHORT STORIES

Urban Fantasy

Eternally Late

Dealings With Joe

Glimpses (short story in That Moment When Anthology)

Contemporary

The Brat Next Door

Fantasy LitRPG

(Set in the same world as Guardians Of The Round Table Series)

Tales Of Inadon 1: The Disc (Co-written with Storm and Rhys Petersen) (short story in Game On! Anthology)

Post Apocalyptic Sci-Fi

Compulsive Directive

NONFICTION

A Year Of Weekly Writing Exercises (Creative Writing)

Cooking For Families With Allergies (Cooking) (Co-written with Storm Petersen)

Tell Me A Story, Grandma (Memoir)

For the most up to date details on available titles visit:

www.avrilsabine.com/books/bibliography

Assassins Of The Dead Series

To learn more about this series visit:

www.avrilsabine.com/series/aotd

BOOKS AVAILABLE IN THE ASSASSINS OF THE DEAD SERIES

Book 1: Dark Blade

Book 2: Dragon Touched

Book 3: Society Against Vampires

Book 4: King's Request

Disclaimer

This is a work of fiction. Names, characters, businesses, places, events and incidents are either the products of the author's imagination or used in a fictitious manner. Any resemblance to actual persons, living or dead, or actual events is purely coincidental. The opinions expressed or beliefs held are those of the characters and should not be assumed to be the opinions or beliefs of the author.